Temple Israel Library
Minneapolis, Minn.

Please sign your full name on the above card.

Return books promptly to the Library or Temple Office.

Fines will be charged for overdue books or for damage or loss of same.

DEM90

One Foot Ashore

One Foot Ashore

JACQUELINE DEMBAR GREENE

WALKER AND COMPANY
NEW YORK

First published in the United States of America in 1994
by Walker Publishing Company, Inc.

Published simultaneously in Canada by Thomas Allen & Son
Canada, Limited, Markham, Ontario.

Library of Congress Cataloging-in-Publication Data
Greene, Jacqueline Dembar.
    One foot ashore / Jacqueline Dembar Greene.
       p.   cm.
    Summary: Arriving alone and destitute in Amsterdam in the
spring of 1654, sixteen-year-old Maria Ben Lazar finds refuge and
friendship in the household of the artist Rembrandt and continues
to pursue her desperate search for her parents and her younger
sister. Sequel to "Out of Many Waters."
    ISBN 0-8027-8281-7
    [1. Jews—Netherlands—Amsterdam—History—
Fiction.   2. Rembrandt Harmenszoon van Rijn,
1660–1669—Fiction.]   I. Title.
PZ7.G834On   1994
[Fic]—dc20   93-22961 √
                                               CIP
                                               AC

Printed in the United States of America

10 9 8 7 6 5 4 3 2 1

For Dawn, Erika, Michael, Anique, Gabrielle, Jennifer, Russell, Heather, Sarah, and of course, Piper

Contents

AUTHOR'S NOTE

After publication of my historical novel, *Out of Many Waters*, readers told me they wanted to know more about the two sisters who had been kidnapped from their home in Portugal and sent to work at a monastery deep in the forests of Brazil. That book followed twelve-year-old Isobel Ben Lazar after she and her older sister, Maria, escaped and stowed away on two ships heading for the distant shores of Amsterdam in the Netherlands.

One Foot Ashore is Maria's story. It begins at the same moment in April 1654, when the sisters escape from the friars who held them, but leads Maria to a different destiny. She steps onto the dock in Amsterdam certain that she will be reunited with Isobel and that together they will find their parents.

Although the sisters are fictional characters, their stories are rooted in factual events of their time. My research into life in Amsterdam led me through stacks of books and also to a visit to the city itself. I had the chance to wander the streets, which look much as they did three centuries ago, tour several of the curiously narrow, ancient residences, and walk through the gracious home and studio of Amsterdam's most famous painter, Rembrandt van Rijn.

Amsterdam in 1654 was the center of world trade and a haven for immigrants. Many Jewish families fleeing persecution found safety under the tolerant Dutch government. Portuguese refugees built a new synagogue and flocked to hear the inspired sermons of Rabbi Menasseh Ben Israel, a famed Torah scholar.

Across the wide, tree-lined street from the rabbi's home lived his close friend, Rembrandt van Rijn. A world-famous artist in his lifetime, Rembrandt felt unappreciated by his countrymen. Although he was a Calvinist by faith, Rembrandt rebelled against his church's strict rules. He moved to the heart of the city's Jewish quarter and drew support from a small circle of friends. In his bright second-floor studio, he painted dramatic biblical scenes using his Jewish neighbors as models. He believed that only their olive-skinned faces and dark eyes reflected true biblical figures.

From my research into Rembrandt's life, I was able to re-create his gruff but sensitive character, and portray the members of his household. He was a notorious spendthrift, constantly purchasing antiques, paintings, and exotic items to use as props. His house was heavily mortgaged and, in 1654, he faced the threat of bankruptcy. His problems were made worse by the fact that his church would not recognize his common-law marriage and made constant threats against his membership.

I would also like to mention the origin of one more character in the book. The tiny rat, Domingo, is based on one of my son's many small pets. From the day we watched the birth of a litter of thumb-sized, hairless creatures, my initial fear and horror of having a rat in the house began to change. I discovered that rats are clean, friendly, and incredibly smart. Our pet sensed when it was time for my son to arrive home from school. It followed us around the house, came when called, and knew exactly which cabinet held the biscuit treats. When this pet died after two years of antics and friendship, I truly missed it. Domingo is a tribute to the creature who forever changed my view of rodents.

Escape

aria tightened the burlap sack that hung from the rope at her waist and glanced down the rutted dirt road. She could see the friars who had kept her and her sister prisoners at the monastery rushing along in pursuit. Fear quickened her breath as she saw how close they were.

"We must get to the harbor or they'll catch us," she whispered to Isobel. Every Jewish child who had been brought to the monastery dreamed of escaping, but in the six years the girls were held there, only a few dared to try. Every one had been caught, and Maria couldn't forget their harsh punishments.

Now the monastery was far behind in the Brazilian forest. Padre Diego and Padre Francisco had traveled in a lumbering oxcart with the two girls for more than a week before they had reached the coast of Recife. The friars said they were going there to establish a branch of the Inquisition for the Church of Portugal. There was so much work to be done, they had brought Maria and Isobel to help.

After months of fighting, the Dutch settlers in Recife had surrendered their colony to the attacking Portuguese. Maria knew that the defeated colonists would quickly sail for the safety of the Netherlands. Boarding one of the departing ships might be her only chance to escape from the friars who had seized her from her family and brought her to this faraway land. She breathed in the salty sea air.

"We're so close to freedom, Isobel! Can't you just smell it?"

"I'm afraid," Isobel said. "Don't leave me." She pulled at her baggy brown frock where it stuck at her back. Maria saw a reddish brown stain where blood had soaked into the coarse fibers of Isobel's robe. Padre Francisco had kicked Isobel sharply this morning while she slept, and Maria knew the cut must be painful.

She wanted to hold her sister and comfort her, but she held herself back, afraid she would never be able to part. What have I done? she thought. I can't leave her.

Isobel's face was a pale mask of fear, and Maria couldn't bear to look into her eyes. Her sister was only twelve years old. Maria was already a woman at sixteen, but her sister was still a child. Could Isobel take care of herself well enough to board one of the ships preparing to leave the harbor and hide until it docked in Amsterdam?

She tried to put her doubts aside. This wasn't the time to question the plan she had worked out so carefully. This was the time to act. The ships wouldn't hold their anchors for stowaways.

On the road behind, the friars were enveloped in a smoky cloud of dust. A shiver rose along Maria's spine. "It's now that we must part," she announced quietly. Her mind raced with thoughts of her sister's fears. Until last night, Isobel hadn't known Maria expected to separate when they escaped. But there's no way we can both hide on one small ship, Maria reminded herself. I know I'm right.

"It will be harder for the priests to find us if we don't go to the docks together," she said. "They'll be asking the townspeople if they've seen two girls, and if we're not traveling in a pair, it may protect us."

The two frightened girls stood at the edge of the line of shops and stalls that ringed the busy harbor. They had hidden in the bushes near the path while a baker sent his son off to the docks to sell fresh loaves of bread to the passengers. How many weeks would they be at sea without fresh food? Maria clutched her sack. It contained a green wine bottle filled with water, some bread, hard-cooked eggs, green bananas, a bit of dried beef, and a few para nuts. She had prepared the same provisions for Isobel and saw her sister's sack tied tightly to her apron strings. It was certainly not enough food to last the entire voyage, but it was something.

Sounds of the friars' excited shouts roused Maria from her concerns. There was no turning back now. She pointed to the rear of the stalls. "I'll go around the marketplace that way," she whispered. "I'm sure all paths lead to the harbor. You follow the baker's boy." Isobel nodded, but her eyes brimmed with fear.

"Remember not to run," Maria cautioned. Isobel was impetuous, often acting or speaking before she thought of the consequences. Running would attract attention. They had to move calmly and blend into the crowd.

Maria looked at her sister one last time. The memory of Isobel's face would have to sustain her through the long voyage. When the soldiers of the Inquisition had pulled them from their home in Portugal, she promised herself she would never leave her sister. But if they didn't part now, they would never be reunited with their parents. The tears she had fought could no longer be held back. They rolled from her eyes unchecked.

Isobel reached her arms toward Maria for a last embrace, but Maria pulled back. "No," she cried, her voice breaking. "No goodbyes." She turned and rushed toward the path. As she moved away she allowed herself one final look. "Go with God, little sister," she prayed. "Go with God."

The friars' voices grew fainter as Maria stumbled along the path, and the noise of the crowd at the harbor reached her ears. She wiped her tears on the rough wide sleeve of her frock, trying to compose herself. This was my plan, she told herself. I will make it work. There are no second chances.

She forced herself to think ahead. I'll need a way to get on board a ship. As she passed behind a fruit stall, a row of large, round baskets filled with green bananas caught her eye. She glanced around to make sure no one was watching and grabbed one of the heavily laden baskets.

The road opened onto the crowded dock. In the harbor, ships' masts rose into the cloudless April sky and Dutch flags waved proudly from their sterns. Colonists elbowed their way into the crowd, anxious to board the ships that would leave the shores of Recife behind. Surely some were Jewish settlers, but many more would be Calvinists. When she had traveled from the monastery, she heard Padre Diego call the Dutch dangerous infidels. That was what they called everyone who did not follow the Catholic faith. If Jews or Calvinists stayed in Recife, the friars of the Inquisition would imprison them all.

She remembered hearing her father say that the Dutch government tolerated all religions. Truly that was freedom. Her family had never been free as long as they had been forced to hide their Jewish faith from the Inquisition in Portugal.

But Papa was arranging for us to live in Amsterdam. I am certain he and Mama left for the Dutch city after the soldiers took us away. That was Papa's plan before we were kidnapped. He would have had more reason to leave Portugal once we were gone. Soon we'll all be together again and be free to be Jews without fear.

Once again Maria heard the shouts of the friars, only now they were mixed with the calls of street vendors. "Fresh bread!" shouted the lanky boy she had seen with the baker. "Hot bread!"

"Runaways!" yelled a deep voice that sent a cold chill into Maria. "Girls in monks' frocks! Runaways!"

"*Or*-anges and *pine*-apples!" sang a white-haired man as he pushed a wheelbarrow heaped with fruit. "Don't leave shore without *or*-anges and *pine*-apples!"

Maria lifted the basket of bananas to her shoulder and hid her face behind it. She moved into the crowd of people balancing unwieldy bundles and struggling toward the gangplank. Maria jostled for a position in the moving stream and stole glances at the women around her. The white collar and apron she had secretly sewn for herself and Isobel helped disguise her baggy friar's frock, but her outfit was clearly different from those around her. Her toes showed at her open

sandals, while others wore thick wooden clogs or delicate leather slippers. The women's dresses were tight
around the bodice and embroidered with designs of
flowers or birds. On every head was a crisp white linen
cap. But Maria knew she and Isobel couldn't possibly
look like Dutch colonists. She only hoped to avoid re-
sembling one of the friars.

She stepped onto the long wooden gangplank,
which swayed dangerously under the weight of the
crowd. She could still hear the friars' cries. If recognized, she would be turned over to them instantly.

"Look out for runaways!" rumbled an angry voice on
shore. "Girls in frocks!"

The families around her didn't even turn their
heads. They must hate the Portuguese who have forced
them to leave their homes. Hopefully, they'll have no
interest in helping the Inquisition recapture children.

As she neared the open deck, Maria saw her next
hurdle. One Dutch sailor stood at each side of the
gangplank questioning passengers and motioning them
in various directions. She stepped up to the sailor near-
est her and pointed to the basket.

"*Banana,*" she announced in Portuguese, hoping the
quaver in her voice would not betray her.

One of the sailors leaned closely into her face and
smiled. He said something that made his companion
laugh, then motioned her toward the front deck.

Maria hurried away, her heart pounding. She had
come so far, but she was not safe yet. She looked
around. Where could she hide? There was no time to
waste, for the sailors obviously expected her to deliver
the bananas and return to shore. The thick weave of
the basket cut into her shoulder, and her fingers were

stiff from gripping its rough rim. Everything about her seemed a confusing maze of ropes, lines, and rigging.

As she hurried toward the bow, she bumped into a burly sailor, scattering her bananas across the slippery deck. A stream of angry words rushed from his mouth.

"Desculpe," she apologized in Portuguese. But the sailor did not seem to understand her. He berated her in a loud voice, and Maria feared he would alert the entire ship to her presence. She stopped to pick up the bananas and offered him a small bunch.

His bluster evaporated. He stuffed the bananas into his jacket and marched off. It was a small bribe to pay for being left alone, but she was still frightened.

"God of Isaac, God of Jacob, God of my fathers, help me," she prayed. She scooped up the basket and looked around. A doorway just ahead stood open to the breeze that made the ropes swish and whisper above her head. She walked forward cautiously and peered inside. The room was empty.

She hesitated, then stepped in. An open stove stood beside a bricked oven, and black iron pots hung from a wooden table. A massive oak water barrel with a thick spigot was wedged into a corner. This was no place to hide. Maria flinched as a fat brown and white rat trotted across the floor. She quickly turned away to seek a different shelter.

But then she noticed that the rat gripped a plump white bean in its mouth. Where had the rodent found it? There was no food in the tiny cook room. She looked in the direction the rat had come from and saw a low wooden door, slightly ajar. She set the basket of bananas on the floor and cautiously pushed the door open. Crates of fresh oranges arranged in ragged rows gave a shock of bright color to a small, dim storage room. Water barrels lined one wall, and bulging burlap sacks were piled to the rough beams along the low ceiling. So that's where the bean came from.

She ducked her head and stepped inside. A salty breeze blew through an open wooden porthole and mingled with the sweet smell of oranges. Maria peered behind a tower of sacks. Perhaps there was enough space to make a narrow hideaway. But would she be discovered too soon? Surely the cook would use up those provisions before the end of the voyage. She surveyed the arrangement of orange crates on the wall opposite the porthole. Fresh fruit would spoil in a few weeks, so it was likely those would be gone first. She wouldn't risk hiding there.

Then Maria looked at the wooden casks that stood in a tight double row, their thick spigots waiting to be tapped. She doubted anyone would move those. They must have been arranged so water could be drawn without shifting them. She realized that the barrels were wedged against a sloping beam just to the right of the porthole. The ceiling was so low that they couldn't be pushed all the way to the wall. Behind the barrels were a stack of buckets, a pile of empty burlap sacks, and a few full bags stamped with the letters BONEN.

The thud of a heavy object hitting the deck in the cook room frightened Maria into action. She quietly eased the stack of buckets aside and slipped into the narrow opening behind the barrels just as a sailor shuffled into the storage room. Maria pulled an empty sack over her and flattened herself against the lumpy bags on the floor. Her heart thumped against her chest as the covering of the porthole slammed shut and the room was plunged into darkness. Maria heard the sailor leave the storage area and close the door. She sat up and strained to pick up every sound. Outside the cook room, Maria heard the unmistakable click of a padlock. Then there was silence.

I am locked in, she realized. Then this will have to be my home for the voyage. Maria made out the shape of the rat slipping between the barrels and disappearing behind a stack of food sacks at the back of the room. It seems I am not alone, but sharing my room with a rat will only make me feel like I'm back at the monastery, she reasoned. If I'd gained one day of freedom for every rat that scurried across the floor or surprised me in the pantry, I'd have been free years ago. And after all, it's that brown and white thief I have to thank for leading me here.

Maria took two buckets from the pile in front of her. I'll try to use one of these to hold wash water, and I'll need the second one, too. At least I know where the outhouse is on a ship. She pushed some of the sacks toward the opening, knowing she would need more protection from anyone entering the storage room. The sacks were heavy, but she pushed and rolled until she had piled up three of them. Then she remembered the bananas. I shouldn't have left them for the cook. She hung her own bag of food from a nail above her, and then climbed over the barrier she had constructed.

Bending low to avoid hitting her head, Maria moved silently through the darkness. She knew she would be safe from discovery as long as the cook room door was locked from the outside. She reached toward the basket and grabbed a large bunch of bananas. Then she nudged the storage door until it closed with a soft click.

Following along the row of barrels, Maria eased herself back into her makeshift hideaway. She pushed into a shadowy corner, clutching the green bananas against her and listening to the sounds of the ship. Wood rubbed against wood, ropes slapped together, men shouted gruffly. Her muscles tensed when she heard heavy boots gathering on deck. Then she recognized the creak and groan of the anchor being lifted as the sailors chanted in rhythm to their work.

The last time I heard that sound was on the ship that carried me and Isobel from Portugal and brought us to this lonely land. I hated that foul ship, but I welcome this one. This time I've *chosen* to cross the ocean. If only I could have kept Isobel with me.

Little sister, I pray you are safe. We are on separate ships, but we sail together. And when we set our feet on shore, we'll be a family again.

2

In Hiding

erk! Werk! Werk!" muttered a deep voice. Maria was startled awake. Someone was in the storage room. The porthole creaked open and early-morning light made shadows against the water barrels that shielded her. She lay still under the scratchy burlap bag she had used as a blanket. Slowly, cautiously, she inched her foot closer under its protective covering.

For once, Maria thought, my brown frock is useful. If any of it sticks out at the edges of the sack, it isn't likely to be noticed. Both the sack and her friar's robe seemed to be cut from the same brown cloth. She hoped that if the sailor looked behind the water barrels, he would think she was just another bag of dried beans.

The intruder gave a grunt and Maria heard water splash against water. She guessed he might be emptying a bucket he'd used for washing pots. Apparently the porthole was a handy waste chute.

The wooden cover slammed shut and Maria relaxed as she heard the footsteps shuffling back to the next room and the door closing behind them. She poked her head out from under the sack and tried to adjust to the dimness as she heard the clatter of pots in the next room.

I've got to move about while I'm alone, she thought. She was too tall to stand in the low-ceilinged space. She pushed onto her hands and knees, stretching her arms and back forward like a cat rousing itself from a long nap.

Then, sitting cross-legged, she reached for her own supply of food. She uncorked the green bottle and took a small drink of water. Using one of the buckets she had put aside, she carefully held one hand over the bucket and poured a few drops of the previous water over it. She rubbed her hands together and tried to wash her face and neck, making sure any stray drops fell into the bucket to be used again. I have no soap, she thought, but at least the water will help me stay clean.

The ship rose and fell, sailing forward against the slap of the waves. Maria's head felt light with the constant motion.

I won't let myself become dizzy with the boat's rocking, she told herself. I'll simply get used to it. As if to defy the ship's roll and pitch, she pulled a hard-cooked egg from her sack and peeled the shell into the second bucket. This pail will be for waste, she decided.

Maria savored the dry, rubbery egg, making each mouthful last as long as she could. She hadn't eaten since breakfast at the church in Recife. She broke off small pieces of crusty bread and chewed each mouthful thoughtfully.

Isobel and I took this bread from the ovens, she remembered. Maria could still picture the kindly friar

who had given the sisters the extra loaves. He didn't
know this bread would feed us after we escaped. Then
Maria thought of Isobel. *I hope you are breaking bread
with me, little sister.*

In the darkness of her tiny space, Maria brushed up
the fallen crumbs and dropped them into the waste
bucket. Then she pulled it under her, balancing
against the ship's constant rocking, and used it to re-
lieve herself.

There's more privacy here than at the monastery,
she thought. *And no flies. Maybe they don't like ships,
either.*

Maria quietly pushed the stack of clean buckets aside
and edged out of her space. Her heart raced as she listened to the rattling sounds in the next room. *This
isn't a safe time to move about, but I've got to empty
this bucket,* she thought. *I'll dump it out through the
porthole, but I can't let the cover slam or I'll be heard.*

She ran her hands along the outline of the porthole
until she felt its metal latch. Muffling the sound of its
opening with the bottom of her frock, she slowly
pushed the wooden flap open. The door was heavy. Too
heavy to hold it open with one hand and empty the
bucket at the same time. But in the light that entered
the opening, Maria saw a long, brass hook attached to
the frame. A round loop on the cover seemed designed
to hold it in place. She fixed the hook into the loop
and was pleased to see that it held the cover sturdily.

Quickly Maria reached for the waste bucket and
emptied its contents into the sea. She tried to rinse the
bucket in the ocean spray that splashed against the side
of the ship.

As she reached to lower the wooden cover, Maria

could not help gazing at the wide expanse of ocean that surrounded her. Along the horizon she saw the sails of the other ships that traveled to Amsterdam. They billowed forward like white doves proudly puffing out their chests. From this distance the ships seemed to glide along smoothly, as if the ocean were a sheet of blue silk.

Which ship are you on, Isobel? If only I could see you peering through a porthole and know you are safe!

The click of the storage door latch caught Maria by surprise. She froze. Someone was coming in! She tried to close the porthole, but the hook was wedged tightly and she couldn't dislodge it quickly enough. She heard the door creak open. She had to hide—but where? She had moved away from her safe niche to reach the port-hole. Without a moment to think, Maria dove behind a tower of bulging sacks piled next to the opening. She crouched in fear, wondering if the sailor who entered would search carefully to find who had opened the porthole.

Maria peered through a tiny space between two sacks of bags. She saw the figure of an aproned man stooped under the low beams. It had to be the ship's cook. He looked at the opening before him and scratched at his gray beard.

"Hmph." He shuffled forward and unlatched the thick wooden cover, slamming it shut. He muttered to himself, and Maria could only imagine what he said. She prayed the cook would leave the storage room and not investigate further. Maybe he thinks he forgot to close it himself.

But the cook had come in for supplies and had not forgotten his mission. Just above Maria's head, his two strong hands grasped a heavy sack and slid it from the pile. How many sacks would the cook take? Maria was grateful for the return to darkness and thankful the sound of her thumping heart couldn't echo through the storage room as it seemed to echo in her chest.

She heard the man grunt as the bag slid onto his shoulder, and then she heard his boots shuffling back toward the cook room. When she heard the door safely close, she fell back weakly. But a rustle of movement nearby frightened her again. She turned to make out the dim shape of the rat as it scurried deeper into a corner.

I've stumbled into the rat's nest, Maria thought in alarm. Why, it could have bitten me! What if I'd cried out while the cook was here? She knew she would have been caught. They may find me before the end of the voyage, she reasoned, but the farther we are from the shores of Recife, the safer I'll be. At least they couldn't send me back.

She listened to the sound of a knife rapidly chopping against a wooden block in the cook room. Whack, whack, whack. Maria crawled from behind the sacks and inched past the closed porthole. She picked up her empty waste bucket and slid back into the nest she had made for herself. She huddled against the wall, trying to calm herself and blinking into the darkness.

3

Small Companions

he dull clicking of the rat's nails on the wooden floor caught Maria's interest. She blinked, trying to make out more than dim shapes around her. If only she could see in the dark, like the rat that shared her hiding place in the small storage room.

Maria had slept little in the past two weeks, frightened at every sound and tossing uncomfortably on the lumpy sacks beneath her. Tonight the continued activity of the brown and white rat kept her awake. It waddled back and forth from a hole it had chewed in a bean sack to a store of food it was setting up behind the bags near the porthole. Maria would not forget how she had hidden in that same space when the cook nearly discovered her that first morning. Usually the rat carried food, but this time it gripped a ragged piece of burlap in its mouth.

The cook room was silent and Maria knew it was nighttime. After several days hidden in the storage room, she had learned the routines of the ship and the habits of the cook. At dawn he opened the porthole, and in the morning light removed the supplies he needed for the day. After that came a morning of chopping and cooking until the sailors crowded at the cook room door for a meal. There was always a chance after they were served that the cook would return to the storeroom to draw beer from the casks that lined her hiding place, or to retrieve a forgotten item. But he never forgot to shut the porthole, leaving her in darkness. Next she would hear him scouring pots and hanging them with an echoing clang. Sometimes he prepared the morning meal before he left in the evening, leaving it bubbling on the stove overnight. But always, he locked the cook room door behind him each evening, and then Maria felt safe. She was alone to move about, breathe in the sea air at the porthole, and take care of her own needs. But the days moved slowly, and when Maria heard the passengers' children laughing and playing on deck, she felt more and more lonely.

She emerged from her hideaway, propped the porthole open to let in the dim moonlight, and followed the rat with curiosity. Peering over the dwindling pile of food bags, she watched the furry creature busily arranging the cloth in a tentlike fashion. When at last it finished its task, it hunched strangely beneath the burlap, its head poking out and its eyes staring like beads of glass.

Maria was about to return to her own makeshift bed when she saw the rat arch its back with a shudder. It reached back beneath the cloth, holding a tiny pink object in its mouth. What could it be? She leaned closer, being careful not to scare the animal, but it seemed to take no notice of her. The rat licked the still object vigorously until it began to squirm.

It's a baby, she realized with surprise. The pear-shaped rodent had waddled about the storeroom not because it was fat, but because it was about to have babies. The mother rat nudged the hairless, wrinkled baby toward her middle, where it began to nurse hungrily. Then she arched her back, reached behind her, and pulled forth another newborn. Maria was captivated by the methodical way in which the mother delivered each infant, licked it clean, and set it to nurse. She repeated her miraculous feat until seven unseeing babies nestled into her warmth. As they safely snuggled against her, the mother stretched out wearily. The burlap cloth sheltered them all, rising and falling slightly with their rapid breathing.

Maria dragged a large sack in front of the rat's bed, making sure the animals were hidden from view. Then she added a few pieces of banana to the rat's pile of beans. "Rest, little mama," she whispered. "You'll be safe here."

Maria quietly closed the porthole and curled up in her own hiding place, feeling a contentment she could not explain. She heard a stiff breeze slapping at the sails, but she slept undisturbed by the sudden pitched roll of the ship and the clatter of pots swinging against each other in the nearby cook room.

When she next opened her eyes the ship was crashing into heavy waves and rain pelted the wooden deck outside. Sails whipped in the wind, and she heard the urgent shouts of sailors on deck. The ropes that had brushed lazily against the railings and masts when she had boarded the ship now creaked and groaned as if straining to break free. Maria's stomach churned as she struggled to get up, steadying herself against the piles of sacks around her. She moved cautiously to the porthole, pushing it open just enough to peer out. A cold rain blew against her face and she could see nothing except white foam that sprayed against the ship. She drew back just as the ship pitched violently, nearly

knocking her down and slamming the cover shut.
Crates of oranges tumbled from their stacks and sent
fruit rolling and bouncing across the floor.

We're caught in a storm! She feared the ship would
overturn, spilling everything into the sea. But I can't
swim, she thought. Then Maria remembered the animals that shared her space. I wonder if the babies are
all right. At least rats can swim. But surely the babies
are too small and weak to survive such huge waves.

A wave of nausea roiled Maria's stomach and sent a
sour bile into her mouth. Rushing to the porthole, she
propped it open and began vomiting what little food
she had eaten. For hours she leaned into the cold wet-
ness, pelted by rain and splashing spray, retching until
her raw throat gagged on emptiness.

As the driving rain gave way to thick gray fog, she
closed the wooden cover once again and crept back to her
hideout. Every limb ached and her stomach churned with
sharp pains. She closed her eyes in exhaustion. Was it her
imagination, or did the ship seem to ride the waves more
gently? Dear God, let the storm pass.

A shrill whistle sounded on deck, calling the morning crew. It must be dawn. She heard the lock on the
cook room door click open, and then the sound of water splashing into a metal pan. If the cook was preparing breakfast, the storm must be over. Otherwise, the
pots would spill, and the sailors couldn't think of leaving their posts. The ship rose and fell in rhythm, and
the waves seemed to break in front of the bow instead
of crashing over it.

Quietly Maria stole across the room to where the
rats nestled. She knew it was risky with the cook at
work, but she had to see if they were safe. The mother

lay on her side and the babies pawed each other for a place to nurse. The cloth had fallen, and Maria cautiously replaced it over the babies, fearing the damp air would chill them. She watched them grope about blindly, climbing over their siblings, seeking warmth. When at last they slept in a ragged pile against their mother, Maria returned to her bed. She pulled two musty bags over her damp frock and tried to warm her shivering body. Then she gave in to the weariness that gripped her, and slept.

Days passed and Maria watched the tiny rats as they opened their eyes to the world. Their stubby tails began to grow longer and downy fur sprouted on their pink bodies. Some of the babies became adventuresome, crawling away from the pack for brief inspections of their surroundings, but always returning to snuggle up to their mother for nourishment and security. Their dark eyes watched Maria without fear. As she realized they would not hurt her and that the mother rat tolerated her presence, Maria became braver. At first she only stroked their soft fur timidly, but soon she began picking them up in her hands.

As the babies grew, the mother rat began leaving them for longer periods. She sauntered off to follow her own secret passages, sometimes returning with a morsel of food in her mouth. Maria wondered if the passengers below deck were finding their own supplies tapped by the fearless rat. The nights were filled with busy activity, but the animals slept during the day.

Maria had adopted their habits, finding it safer to be silent during the day while the cook worked, and giving her more freedom at night when the cook room was deserted. Then she could open the porthole, and in the light of the evening stars she learned to scavenge for food, just like the mother rat. Some nights she stole fresh oranges, and others she sneaked into the cook room itself and filled up on dry biscuits.

One morning as the first rays of rosy light began to line the horizon, Maria realized that the mother rat had not returned. She closed the porthole and retreated to her shelter, but stayed awake, listening for the familiar clicking sound when the rat trotted across the floor. She held her breath as the cook performed his expected chores and then closed the door of the storeroom. Then the only noise she heard was the complaining squeals of the babies as they sought their mother's milk.

They've got to eat, she thought. She heard the shuffling sounds of crewmen lining up for bowls of porridge. If I move around now, the sailors might hear me. And there's always the chance that the cook might come back. But if I don't feed the babies, the sailors might come to investigate their squeaking.

Maria listened to be certain the cook was still occupied with serving the food, then moved silently across the narrow room. The babies were crawling around in a frantic search for their mother. Maria took an orange from the bin and returned to her niche. She removed a curved section of the orange rind and filled it with water from her bottle. She pulled a hard biscuit from her sack and crumbled a piece into the makeshift bowl of water.

This should be soft enough for you little ones to eat, she thought. Then she moved back to the babies' nest. She picked up each one in turn, setting it around the edge of the food. The babies reached toward the water and began washing their paws and faces vigorously. Your mother has given you good manners. Now you can eat.

The noses of the baby rats twitched as they sniffed at the unfamiliar food. Maria was anxious to get back to the safety of her hiding place, but she had to reassure herself that the babies would eat. Finally, the one with a brown triangle of fur on its back picked up a soggy crumb and began nibbling it. The others then grabbed at the floating biscuit pieces, upsetting the orange peel. Water seeped into the sack underneath, but the crumbs remained. Maria knelt on the bumpy sack, watching until they ate every crumb and then huddled into a furry, breathing pile to sleep.

The smallest rat in the litter was the only one who had not found its way into the group. It shivered at the edge of the bean sack, as if uncertain where to go. Maria scooped him up gently in her hands and held him close, trying to warm him. You miss your mama, just like I miss mine. The baby nuzzled against her contentedly, and she offered it a sopping piece of biscuit and then placed it back with its siblings. Maria dropped the ragged piece of burlap over them and stole back to her own lumpy bed.

Where are you, little mama? Did you find a better store of food below deck with the passengers? Or did one of the ship's cats find you before you made your way back? I hope you are safe.

When she slept, Maria did not dream of baby rats. She dreamed instead that she was taking care of Isobel, feeding her biscuits and oranges in the dim storage room of a tossing ship.

4

Night Watch

An insistent tugging at her hair roused Maria from sleep.

"Ouch! Stop pulling!" she whispered, as her eyes met the gleaming brown eyes of the tiny rat that tugged at her tangled hair. Maria reached for the furry animal and held him in her hand.

"You are as punctual as the sun," she observed. "Or should I say, the moon?" Her hand stroked the silky brown and white fur of the baby rat. "I know you're all hungry, Domingo. Your humble servant is about to prepare your evening meal."

It had been nearly a month since the mother rat had failed to return from her nighttime foraging, a month since Maria had cared for the babies left behind, feeding and protecting them.

Maria stretched her stiff back and surveyed the squirming nest of tiny rats she had placed near her on a flour sack. If she had to care for them, she could not risk crossing the storage room too often, so she had moved them into her hiding place. Here she could feed them each night and be certain they didn't stray into the cook's path. Tonight they made soft mewling noises as they clambered over each other in search of food.

Watching them grow had amused her during the long silent hours. As she observed them more closely, she began to identify each baby by the shape of the brown patches that stood out against its white fur. Soon she found that each one seemed to have a distinct personality. Before long she named the seven squealing babies after the days of the week.

The playful ball of fur who awakened her tonight was Domingo. He was the smallest of the litter and the sleepiest. "That is why I named you for Sunday," Maria told him in a hushed voice. "Domingo is the last day of the week, and that's the only day the friars at the monastery ever let us get a bit of rest."

She dropped Domingo into the nest with his brothers and sisters and filled a wooden saucer that she had pilfered from the cook room with water from her green bottle. From her sack she withdrew a few dry white beans and dropped them into the water to soften. Then she took a chunk of dry biscuit and broke it into small pieces around the dish. The babies pushed and shoved until they had each found a space. They would be able to eat the biscuit now, and later on the beans would become soft enough for them to nibble.

"Now let's see what the cook has left for the stowaway," she whispered. She moved to the low doorway and listened for a few moments before easing the door open. As it was every night, the cook room was locked tight from the outside and Maria was alone. She sniffed the air. Once, a vegetable stew was left simmering overnight and she had savored the hot broth rich with the mingled flavors of carrots, turnips, and onions. At other times there had been a thick bean soup. But usually there was only a pot of sticky, dark porridge. When the seas were rough, the cook left nothing behind, and Maria had to be content with stale biscuits.

As her eyes adjusted to the shadowy darkness, Maria saw steam puffing from a giant pot on the stove. She wrapped her hand in her apron and lifted the hot cover. A thick wheatmeal bubbled before her. It certainly would be pasty and tasteless, but it was hot and nourishing, and she tried to be grateful for it.

She set the lid back, being careful that the handle at its center was aimed in the same direction as when she had found it. She began to make a mental picture of every item in the room. A long-handled ladle hung from a nail in the wall. Maria had used it before to scoop a few mouthfuls of whatever was cooking, but she had to be sure to replace it exactly. She noted that the bowl of the ladle was facing the wall tonight, and that the handle hung just behind the nail head. She would remember that.

There was a bucket of wash water next to the worktable, and Maria was relieved to see that the dirty water had not yet been tossed out of the porthole. That made it easier for her to clean the ladle after she used it. I wonder why he left in such a hurry tonight. He hasn't even thrown the wash water into the sea.

After swallowing a few ladlefuls of porridge, she washed the utensil carefully, wiped all traces of water on her frock, and hung it back on the nail exactly as she had found it. The crates of fresh oranges that had filled the storage room with their sweet smell had been used up weeks ago, and the small supply of food in Maria's bag had lasted only a few days. Sacks of dried beans remained and a few untapped barrels of water and beer, but the fresh food was gone. Maria was sick of the musty ship and her cramped quarters. She prayed the dwindling supplies signified that the voyage was nearing its end.

She took a few swallows from her water bottle and then refilled it under the spigot of the water barrel. When it was again full and corked, she bent down and carefully wiped the drops that had splashed onto the floor.

The night was calm and Maria could feel the boat rise and fall in rhythm. She shuddered as she remembered the storm they had weathered a few weeks ago. A wave of dizziness passed over her as she thought of how ill she had been, and how frightened. The wind and waves had battered the wooden hull, and the ship had tossed about like a leaf in a whirlpool.

Maria steadied herself against the worktable until the feeling of dizziness passed. I am not made for traveling on ships. I hope the journey is nearly over and I can soon plant my feet on solid earth again.

She looked around the room, noting every detail, and making certain she had left nothing amiss. The pot bubbled against the lid, the ladle hung from its nail, and everything was as it had been. Maria turned to go back to the storage room when her knee banged one of the iron pots that hung from the worktable. She stifled a cry as the pain jangled up her leg. Quickly she muffled the pot with her hands as it clanged noisily into its mates. But she had not reacted fast enough. The sound of heavy boots approached the door. Her clumsiness had alerted a night watchman. She froze, uncertain whether to move into her hiding place or stand still so as not to risk making any more noise. Her heart thumped as he pulled at the door lock.

She slipped into the storage room and hid behind the open door. There was a loud rattle as the heavy lock swung back, and then the sound of boots moving slowly away. Maria let out her breath.

She silently opened the porthole, settled back into the pile of bean sacks, and tucked her feet under her. The rats had eaten all the biscuit and had gnawed some of the beans. Their little teeth were developing. Soon they would be able to take care of themselves. She took some satisfaction in knowing that she had nurtured them and that they were healthy and growing. *If I ever told anyone I cared for a litter of rats, they would think me crazy, but these gentle creatures have kept me alert and given me something to care about. People shouldn't despise them simply because they are rats. Didn't God make us all?*

Maria had cared for the babies ever since their mother had disappeared. They had become used to her, nuzzling her fingers with their warm pink noses and allowing her to pick them up. But it was Domingo who rubbed against her cheek or pulled playfully at her long hair. Only Domingo left his brothers and sisters in a sleepy pile to cuddle in the folds of her frock.

Tonight the rats explored the storage room, pulling themselves energetically up and down the burlap sacks and poking into dark spaces. But Domingo scrambled onto Maria's lap as soon as she sat down. The moonlight seemed to make his sleek fur glow, and she couldn't resist reaching out to him.

"When you were born, you looked like the tip of my thumb after I did the friars' washing." Domingo

grasped her finger between his front paws and began to
lick it. Even in the semidarkness, Maria could see his
delicate pink fingers that made her think of a baby's
hands.

"You would have liked our house in Portugal," she
whispered. Domingo stopped his industrious licking
and looked up at the sound of her voice. "Isobel and I
played in big sunny rooms with shiny red tiles on the
floors and a flower garden in the center courtyard. And
there was so much food in the kitchen. Whenever we
wandered in, the cook gave us *biscochos* to eat. They're
delicious twisted cookies with sesame seeds sprinkled
on top. You wouldn't have to eat stale biscuits there
and I would never eat porridge! When I looked out the
windows, I could see the gates of the Royal Palace. You
see, my father is Abraham Ben Lazar, and he was the
king's most trusted adviser in matters of state." Domingo played with the folds of her apron, hiding underneath, then popping out in different spots.
"Doesn't that sound important, 'matters of state'?"

Maria thought back to the life she had led before she
and Isobel had been kidnapped and taken to Brazil.
She knew it couldn't have been as perfect as she remembered. Of course, she knew that the Holy Inquisition dominated the people, constantly searching for
anyone who didn't follow the Church's teachings. And
it was true that those who were judged guilty were put
in prison, or sentenced to death.

"We were *conversos*, little friend," she explained.
"Sometime before even my parents were born, our family was forced to convert and publicly deny our Jewish
faith. For generations we had to pretend to follow the

Catholic religion in order to survive. But behind the walls of our house we were always Jews."

Maria stroked the brown fur that capped Domingo's head and striped his back. "I always felt safe because our family was under the protection of the king. Then everything changed."

The room became darker as the ship changed direction and the moon no longer shone in at the open porthole. She settled against a lumpy sack and closed her eyes for a moment. It seemed as if she had told the story of their capture to Isobel only yesterday, but they had been apart for so many long weeks. Still, she felt as if her sister was close by as she talked to Domingo.

"I'll never forget the night we were kidnapped," Maria told him. The sound of waves splashing in rhythm against the ship lulled her. "Papa was not home, and what could Mama do against the soldiers? I was terrified. I couldn't understand what was happening. I clung to Isobel so they wouldn't separate us. Even after they locked us into the hold of a ship, I truly believed the king would send word. He would tell the captain there had been a mistake and that the children of Abraham Ben Lazar were to be released. But no messenger ever came."

She thought of her one night of seasickness during the recent storm, and knew that she had been lucky. When she and Isobel had sailed from Portugal, they endured weeks of churning stomachs and dizziness. Now she looked down at Domingo and saw his eyes glinting at her. He seemed to like the sound of Maria talking to him.

"When we docked in Brazil, friars put us into oxcarts and took us deep into the jungle to live at a monastery.

There were already other *converso* children there, and each day the priests made us study the church's teachings and learn its prayers. But mostly we worked. You don't know what it's like to pull weeds under the hot sun, or scrub dirty floors on your hands and knees, or endlessly stir a pot in a stifling kitchen. The worst thing isn't even the hard work. It's the loneliness. You know your parents are somewhere, but you are alone."

Maria moved out of her narrow space and gazed through the porthole. A stiff breeze blew at her tangled hair. Domingo hopped along behind her and she lifted him to the opening, where he sniffed the air.

"The night watchmen guard the ship, but we truly watch the night. Do you think the sailors ever look up to see how the stars sparkle like the queen's jewels? Or how the moon seems to sail upon the water?" There was just a hint of brightness at the horizon, and Maria could make out the silhouettes of the companion ships. She recognized that the sky was showing signs of the daylight to come. Balancing Domingo on her shoulder, she closed the porthole and crawled back into the safety of her hidden niche.

"When Isobel and I escaped to the harbor, there were sixteen ships waiting to take the colonists to the safety of Amsterdam. Now we're part of that group. I know that when Isobel and I land in Amsterdam, we will find our parents there. And you'll come, too. I won't leave you, little friend."

5

One Foot Ashore

erhaps it was the change in the ship's rhythm that awakened Maria, but when she opened her eyes, she was drawn to the port-hole by a sound she had not heard since the ship sailed from Recife. It was the shrill, mournful cry of a gull. She pushed the wooden covering open slightly and scanned the brightening sky until she made out the dark silhouette of a lone sea bird hover-ing above the ship, calling out the news that land was near.

Domingo stirred in his sleep, his left foot twitching nervously. He must be dreaming of running. Although I am awake, I'm dreaming of stepping onto shore and finding Isobel and my parents.

Maria eased the porthole cover down and fastened it shut. She settled back into the security of her dark shelter, afraid to risk being discovered in the daylight. She heard the cook talking with the sailors as he ladled their porridge. The morning meal was usually a quiet affair, with wooden bowls rattling and feet shuffling forward in a line. Few words were exchanged. But to-day talk was lively and the voices less gruff.

Maria could not get back to sleep. Like the conversations in the cook room, the sounds of life aboard the ship announced a change. She listened alertly to the rustle of sails being lowered and the clatter of wooden shoes upon the deck. With her night hours and daytime sleeping habits, she had rarely heard the passengers. Perhaps they were now lining up with their belongings, preparing to disembark. As the day advanced, she heard the unmistakable noise of the sailors lowering the ship's anchor. The wooden winch creaked and groaned with disuse, and the heavy chain clanked as it turned. Her curiosity grew until she felt she must see what was happening. She crept back to the porthole and risked one brief look outside. Maria's eyes widened in astonishment. A flat port city stretched in front of her, its dock crowded with ships, its long wooden buildings arrayed in rows as far as she could see.

Maria's heart beat rapidly. She prayed the cook room door wouldn't be locked now. We must be in Amsterdam! She picked up her nearly empty sack and tied it to her apron. It contained nothing but a half-filled bottle of water and two dry biscuits, but she might need them until she and Isobel located her parents. Maria had suffered the voyage with as much patience as she could, but now that she had arrived in port she wanted to run from the ship and shout for Isobel. What could anyone do to her now? Surely they wouldn't throw her in jail now that she was in a free land.

But caution overcame her excitement. She huddled in the storage room, listening to the activity that hummed outside. She tried to comb her fingers through her tangled hair as she thought she heard the wooden gangplank being fitted into place. *Will my parents recognize me? I am dirty and ragged and I am nearly a woman now, not a little girl.*

Feet clattered along the deck mixed with the muffled noise of heavy bundles being dragged along. People's voices crackled with excitement, and Maria heard children laughing.

Isobel and I were children when we left Portugal, but our childhood is gone. Now we must find our parents again. I hope Isobel still has the silver combs. Maria remembered the delicate filigreed hair combs she had been wearing when the soldiers carried her from her home. She had kept them hidden in the seams of her clothes for six years, until the night before she and her sister escaped from the friars. Then she had sewn the combs into Isobel's chemise and told her they might help her parents recognize her. Maria grew more and more anxious at the thought of seeing her mother and father again. First she had to find Isobel.

There was a brief period of silence on the ship, and Maria guessed that the last of the passengers had departed. Then a flurry of activity signaled the sailors securing the ship's ropes. She held her breath as someone opened the storage room door, pushed open the porthole, and then hurried out. *Would the sailors begin removing the empty crates and barrels and carrying them ashore?*

The rats had roused themselves in the sudden brightness, although Domingo simply tucked his head farther into the darkness of his fur and continued to sleep. The other six babies had begun wandering off in different directions, and Maria knew it wouldn't be

long before they made their way out of the storage
room and onto the deck. If the sailors saw them, surely
they would come in to investigate.

The morning faded into afternoon, but still Maria
crouched in her narrow shelter. She didn't want to be
caught. Not now when she was so close. She listened
intently as the sailors called to each other, some laughing roughly. Then their heavy boots thumped across
the gangplank. No one returned to the storage room,
and the ship fell into silence.

As the sun set, Maria determined to make her way
ashore. She weighed the dangers of trying to keep Domingo with her, and then ignored all the reasons for
leaving him behind. She tucked the sleeping animal
into her wide sleeve and cautiously made her way to
the cook room.

Walking softly in her sandals, she looked out the
double door that stood open, just as she had found it
so many weeks ago. The deck seemed deserted and
there was no watch posted. The sails were tied securely
to the masts, and a Dutch flag fluttered aloft. The ship
is home, she thought, and with God's blessing, so am I.

Gripping her sleeve tightly against her wrist, Maria
emerged into the dusky light. She hurried across the
deck and down the gangplank. Her legs wobbled unsteadily as she set her feet on land once again. Sand
and grit caught between her exposed toes. She rubbed
them together to revel in the certain sign that she was
now ashore.

She swallowed hard and folded her arms across her
chest to steady her trembling hands. Now that she had
arrived in Amsterdam, she realized how alone she was.
She hung back in the lengthening shadows of a long

brick building. Blue awnings stretched from its high walls over a row of wooden tables, but the peddlers who sold wares from these stalls had gone home.

A thin crowd of people radiated from the center of the square, carrying bundles and baskets as they made their way toward the narrow streets that wound away from the market. A horse pulled a strange wooden sled piled with pots and pans. It clattered noisily as its flat runners scraped across the bare cobblestones. Maria's shoulders twitched nervously as a rooster crowed an evening cry. She turned and saw its cage being loaded into a rough wheelbarrow next to a crate of cackling hens. Huge barrels were rolled along the docks to a customs house where they were hoisted onto scales. It seemed the ships that sailed from the colony of Recife in Brazil were emptying their holds of lumber, tobacco, sugar, and spices. Now the merchants of Amsterdam would stock the marketplace with goods.

But Maria wasn't interested in the barrels and crates that were hauled from the ships' holds. She waited only for one other passenger to make her way ashore—Isobel. The thought of her young sister made Maria's hands tremble harder and filled her with a fear greater than when she had escaped from Recife. Had Isobel found a safe hiding place on one of the ships before it sailed? It was a question she had asked herself a thousand times in the past few weeks.

I didn't want to leave her alone, she thought, but we had to hide on separate ships. Isobel had cried, but Maria was certain it was the only way for them to escape. She had tried to reassure Isobel that they would be together again in a short time. But the weeks hiding aboard ship had seemed neverending, and now Maria's certainty that they would step ashore at the same moment seemed foolish. If Isobel did sail to Amsterdam, where is she now?

A tickle of movement rustled her wide sleeve. "Don't be afraid, Domingo," she whispered, patting the coarse brown frock. The sleeve bulged with a flutter of activity as Domingo pushed to get out. She continued to pat gently. "Don't be afraid." Then the rat was still.

Maria had hoped that the drab friar's frock she had been forced to wear for so many years might be replaced with a real dress before she arrived in Amsterdam, but there was no chance for that. She tucked its hood inside and tried to smooth her long white apron and collar, but they had become wrinkled and soiled and she knew she must look like a street urchin. Her long black hair was matted and snarled, and her dusty feet showed through her open sandals.

Still, I made it this far. The only thing that matters is finding Isobel. How can I go to my parents without her?

The guttural sounds of Dutch conversations filled the air with a confusing din. She spoke only Portuguese and could not even ask for her sister or her parents. But she hadn't forgotten her father's plan, and she was more certain than ever that her parents would have left Portugal. Once Maria and Isobel had been taken away, it would have been too dangerous to stay. If the king had not protected Papa's children, anything could happen.

The high-pitched chatter of a woman's voice grew clearer as a richly dressed couple walked past the empty stalls. They were speaking Portuguese! Maria took a

tentative step forward, half-emerging from the shadows, trying to decide if she should address them. The
woman wore a tight-waisted lavender gown that rustled
as she walked in delicate, thin-soled slippers. Her dark
hair was pulled back from her face and shiny curls
spilled down her back and across her shoulders. There
were pearls at her throat, above a neckline that fell low
across her bosom. The man at her side wore a large,
wide-brimmed hat. A white plume swooped low across
the brim and rippled against the wind. His tall polished boots clicked smartly against the cobblestones,
and a black cape lined with yellow silk hung casually
from one shoulder and flapped against his leg.

Maria clutched tightly at her sleeve. She did not
want Domingo to poke his head out now. She stepped
forward awkwardly, muttering apologies.

"*Desculpe,*" she began. "Do you know . . ."

The woman pulled back in disgust, holding a delicately embroidered handkerchief to her nose. The man
gripped her elbow, eased her away, and placed himself
between Maria and the lady.

"Get away!" he commanded in Portuguese. "Don't
you know it's against the law to beg on the streets?
We'll have you thrown in jail!" He turned back to his
companion and guided her swiftly away, complaining
angrily. "Such riffraff coming off the boats! Amsterdam is becoming a city of beggars!"

Maria stepped back into the shadows to hide her
shame. They thought she was just a homeless beggar!
But what was she, if not that? She sagged against the
rough bricks of the building. The man was right. She
had no money and no place to call home. She slid

down until she sat on the damp walkway, moving under cover of the wooden table in the corner stall.

"We will have a home," she said with determina-
tion. "Soon, Domingo, we'll find Isobel and Papa and
Mama. We *will* be a family again."

His small pink nose pushed out at the end of Maria's
sleeve, sniffing the air warily. This time she let him
come out to explore. Behind the pointed muzzle were
two sharp black eyes and tiny ears shifting alertly to
catch the slightest sound. She reached for her companion, stroking his sleek fur, and even his nearly hairless
tail. "Such a good little rat. Come, Domingo, come
and see Amsterdam!"

He grasped Maria's finger lightly in his tiny pink
paws, rubbing his rough tongue against her skin.
"You're right, little friend," she said. "I do need a good
cleaning, but it's going to take more than your little
tongue to do it. How I need a bath!" Domingo leaned
back into the crook of her arm, resting as if he were
seated in a soft chair. He continued to lick her finger
while she tickled his belly.

People passed by, but they didn't notice her. The
marketplace was becoming quiet, and the shadows
deepened into darkness. A damp chill crept into the
air and Maria shivered in her thin frock. Domingo
stretched his hind legs and yawned. Then, as if to wake
himself up, he scampered up to Maria's shoulder.

"You must be hungry." She reached down to the
burlap bag. As soon as Domingo saw her loosen it, he
scurried to her lap and stood on his back legs with his
front paws raised in expectation. Maria pulled out a
hard biscuit and broke off a piece. He took it with his
paws, placed it firmly in his mouth, and began to

search for a place to hide. She sheltered him with her arm, and with this sense of security, he again grasped the morsel in his paws and began to nibble hungrily.

A light drizzle began to fall and she pushed closer to the wall, allowing the stall table to shelter her. She pulled her hood out and covered her head. "You and I are survivors, aren't we?" she asked Domingo. The rat sniffed around, searching for fallen crumbs.

"I have lost my mother, just like you. And I left my sister. I pray I didn't do the wrong thing." Domingo snuggled back into her sleeve and curled up, wrapping his tail across his face. Maria gathered a few clumps of straw that had snagged in the spaces between the cobblestones and tried to make a comfortable place to rest her head. The straw smelled faintly of rotten vegetables and mildew, but it was preferable to the hard stones beneath her.

She kept a watchful eye on the deserted marketplace that stretched in front of her. She had walked onto free soil as she had dreamed. But without Isobel, she felt she was still adrift. It was as if only one foot had stepped ashore.

"Tomorrow, Domingo," she whispered softly. "Tomorrow we'll find her."

Searching the Marketplace

hurch bells clanged the hour, piercing the silence of the thick fog that filled the marketplace. It was five o'clock in the morning and Maria welcomed the coming of day. She had been awake through the night, keeping her hands on Domingo as he foraged between the cobblestones. She was used to being alert all night on the ship, but now was the time when she normally curled up in her hiding place and slept. She was tired and her muscles ached with the damp chill, but she was anxious to begin her search for Isobel.

She rubbed her cramped feet and legs. Domingo scampered onto her lap, nudging the apron aside and searching excitedly for the bag of food.

"You're always hungry," she teased. "Except when you're sleeping!" She pulled another hard biscuit from the sack. "I think straw would taste better," she said, giving Domingo his portion.

He ate quickly and began exploring the street for a puddle of water. Maria scooped him up and brought him back to her lap. She did not want the rat to drink dirty water, for she knew he could easily pick up ill-

nesses that might spread. She had watched him each
day since his birth and knew he was healthy and clean
now. She had to be careful to keep him that way. She
uncorked the water bottle and filled her cupped hand.
Domingo scooped up a few drops with his front paws,
washing his face and ears carefully. Then he rested one
pink paw against Maria's hand and began lapping up
the water. She took a few swallows from the bottle and
stored it in her sack. She lifted Domingo up to her
sleeve and he clambered in, ready for a nap now that
his belly was filled.

Maria crawled from beneath the empty stall and
tried to scan the square through the fog. Some peddlers
arrived, perhaps to get the choicest locations from
which to sell their wares, and a few ragged men also
began to emerge from alleys and sheltered alcoves. No
doubt they are people like me, she thought, people
with no home. I hope Isobel has found a hiding place,
too, and will come into the marketplace soon.

Maria began to walk slowly along the edges of the
square, straining her eyes into corners and alleys, looking for a small girl in a brown friar's frock. There were
a few beggars concealed among the buildings and stalls,
their heads and faces covered by strange pointed hats
and their feet wrapped in rags. Maria's heart raced as
she looked them over. Surely they are as harmless as I
am, she tried to reassure herself, just hungry and
lonely. But their tattered clothes made her think they
had lived like this for a long time. Such people would
be desperate.

The vastness of the square surprised Maria. She had
not taken in its size when she arrived last night. She
remembered her astonishment when she first saw the

lively market at the docks in Recife, but it would fit
into just one corner of the square in Amsterdam. Recife was just a tiny colony, but Amsterdam was a huge
city.

More peddlers came into the square. Most were
farmers in coarse clothing who pushed wheelbarrows
filled with vegetables or cages of barnyard animals.
Their thick wooden shoes clopped against the cobbles
and splashed through shallow puddles. Some men and
women had long-stemmed gray pipes protruding from
their lips, and the bittersweet smell of tobacco curled
into the air and mingled with wisps of fog. Maria
looked hopefully into every face she passed, but none
was Isobel's.

A pale orange sun rose across the water, illuminat-
ing the ships that lay at anchor and dissolving the last
hint of darkness. The marketplace was like an anthill
that had just awakened. The slow trickle quickly became a hum of activity. Calls rang out through the
crowd, women's high voices and men's low-pitched
shouts trying to attract buyers. Maria was reminded of
the Bible's story of the Tower of Babel and felt as
though she had been dropped into that mythical place
where every person spoke a different language, and no
one could understand anyone else. All around her she
heard a cacophony of words that held no meaning for
her. But, unlike the Bible story, everyone else in the
marketplace understood the language.

"*Pannekoeken!*" shouted a melodious voice. "*Warm
pannekoeken!*"

A woman sat on a low stool cooking a thick pancake
over an open fire. Her hair was hidden beneath a white
linen cap except for a row of curly blond bangs that

sprang out across her forehead. She had a straw basket of wooden spoons beside her and a clay pitcher filled with fresh batter. She held a black iron frying pan in one hand, its long curving handle wrapped in a thick cloth to protect her from the heat. As Maria watched, the woman gave the pan a practiced flick and the pancake flipped over. The sweet smell of the wood fire and the buttery pancake made her stomach rumble. She longed for a hot meal and a warm place to rest.

A young boy brushed past her and thrust a coin at the pancake seller. She shook a large sprinkle of sugar atop the cake and rolled it tightly into a square of white paper. Maria could not help staring as the boy sauntered off, stuffing his mouth full.

The woman eyed her suspiciously, seeming to guess that her pockets were empty.

"*Weggaan!*" she shouted gruffly, waving Maria off with her free hand. Maria didn't understand the word, but she understood the angry tone of voice. She turned away, remembering that her only mission now was to find Isobel.

Along the fringe of the market three boys stood about idly while an older man struggled to hang a heavy slab of raw meat from a wooden frame. She watched as one of the boys held a fresh animal bladder to his mouth and puffed it full of air while his companions laughed and slapped each other on the back. The thin white skin ballooned into a great ball. As it stretched wide, he suddenly turned in Maria's direction and clapped the bladder against his fist. It burst in the air with a sickening pop, spraying bits of bloodied tissue on Maria's face and clothes. She jumped back in disgust, but the boys only laughed and pointed at her as she moved quickly into the crowd, wiping her face and clothes with her apron.

Now I am dirtier than before, she realized. She felt humiliated and insulted at the same time. She glanced back over her shoulder, afraid the ruffians might be following. I did nothing to them to deserve such a cruel trick. I must find Isobel and get away from this place. She looked carefully at every stall she passed, hoping her sister was somewhere about, but she saw only plump pink faces framed in wispy blond hair. It seems there are no dark-haired children in all of Amsterdam, Maria thought, but that should only make it easier for me to find Isobel.

Maria had moved nearly full circle around the square when she stopped in her tracks, unable to believe what was ahead of her. A pale, hollow-cheeked man dressed in tattered clothes walked among the crowd balancing a long pole against his shoulder. Hanging from the pole were the grotesque forms of dead rats, frozen in tortured positions. She shivered in horror, clutching her sleeve tightly to her body. A wooden box hung from the man's neck on a leather strap. It was marked with a crudely painted skull and crossbones.

Why, he's a rat catcher, and his box is full of poison. A wave of nausea churned Maria's stomach. She hurried from the man's path as he sauntered through the knots of people. He rolled the stick back and forth against his shoulder so the dead rats quivered at the end of their dangling strings. The man's stony gray eyes fixed on Maria and he gave her a frightening smile, filled with crooked, brown, stained teeth.

I'll never let the rat catcher find Domingo. He's mine and I shall protect him.

She began running toward the docks, afraid to stay any longer among the hostile people in the square. She didn't know where she would go now, but she knew she wasn't welcome in Amsterdam. *I expected some kindness from these people, but it seems as if the country's chilly weather has affected their hearts as well.*

She slowed down as she approached the weigh-house, for a small crowd had assembled and they were arguing excitedly in Portuguese. She hung back at the fringe of the group, trying not to attract attention. At last here were people she could understand. She didn't want to be chased away before she learned what had caused the commotion. Maybe there was someone in the group with information about her family.

A short, round woman jabbed her finger angrily toward a well-dressed man who towered imposingly above the crowd. She shouted to be heard above the other voices.

"Where is it?" she yelled, her voice filled with agitation. "Where?"

"Yes!" agreed the crowd. "Where's the ship?"

The tall man shrugged and his long cloak rippled with the movement. "It happens frequently," he said. "There is always danger in such voyages. There were sixteen ships leaving port in Recife, but . . ."

Maria stiffened. They were talking about the ships that had taken her from Brazil. Sixteen ships had anchored in the harbor ready to sail on the morning she and Isobel had escaped from the friars and stolen aboard. What had happened? She strained forward, trying to hear.

"But it is impossible to guarantee that all will arrive safely. There was a storm at sea. When it passed and the captains took stock of their position, they realized one ship had been lost."

A young woman holding a chubby-cheeked baby in her arms began to sob. The child echoed its mother's sadness, letting out a loud wail.

"Ay, *meu marido,*" she lamented. "My husband!"

Other women in the crowd began to cry, some leaning against each other for support. A portly man dressed in modest but finely tailored clothes spoke up.

"Some of us had a great financial investment in *The Valck* and its cargo," he said, "and some had something more precious—members of our family. To say that the ship is lost is simply not enough. Was there any sign that it sank during the storm? Is it possible that it has simply been set off course and will show up in the next few days?"

"We haven't lost hope," the tall man said, "but we must recognize the seriousness of the situation. The ship could have been damaged badly, and unable to resume its journey. And there is always the possibility of privateers." There was a murmur of shock among the people.

"Ay, privateers!" cried the woman with the wailing baby.

"The seas are dangerous," declared the man, with no trace of emotion. "All I can suggest is that you return to your homes and contact us again in a few weeks. If we have further news, of course we will share it with you."

The official tried to move away, but the people in the crowd followed on his heels, shouting and waving their arms. Maria let them pass her by. She didn't know which ship her sister had boarded, and there was

no proof that she was hidden on *The Valck*. But somehow she had a feeling that Isobel's fortunes were tied
to the fate of that ship.

Maria sagged against short wooden piles that pro-
truded from the dock. As the official had said, she had
to face the situation. She could hope that Isobel had
arrived safely in Amsterdam, but her hopes would not
change things. Now her task would be to find her parents and tell them what she had done. She had broken
her own vow never to separate from Isobel, and now
her sister was lost. Even if her parents forgave her, Maria couldn't forgive herself. Her eyes brimmed with
tears that spilled down her cheeks.

I shouldn't have let the crowd go without asking for
my parents. If there are Portuguese in this city, surely
they know Abraham Ben Lazar. I should have spoken
up while there were people who would understand me.
Now I can't find my parents, either.

A loud group of boys came running into the square
dogging the steps of a young man rolling a big hoop
across the bumpy cobblestones. He pushed it with a
short stick, keeping it balanced and rolling. The boys
whooped and yelled, waving schoolbooks in the air as
they ran.

Maria turned her back on the boisterous group. She
wanted no more encounters with Amsterdam boys.
She faced the ocean and raised her sleeve to wipe her
eyes dry, when she was suddenly stung by a hard object
that slammed into her back. She gasped and jumped
up from her spot against the piles, nearly losing her
balance. Domingo rustled excitedly in her sleeve, and
Maria tried to keep it closed tightly against her wrist.
She heard loud, unintelligible jeers as the boys who

had been chasing the hoop now swarmed around her, yelling and pointing. What was the word the pancake seller used to chase her away?

"Weggaan!" she shouted at them, but instead of running off, they hooted and howled and laughed all the more. I guess I didn't get the word right, she worried. Another rock was thrown, this one landing on her arm. Domingo gave a frightened squeak, and she crossed her arms protectively across her chest, trying to shelter him. She tried to get away, but the boys surrounded her, blocking her path.

One pulled at her hood, which she had carelessly left untucked. She jerked free only to encounter another boy, who thrust his face close to her and shouted. His breath smelled strongly of dried fish. She didn't know what he said, but his mouth formed an ugly sneer, and his tone was insulting.

Another stone smacked into the back of Maria's head, sending her sprawling across the slippery stones, her arms flying out as she fell. She landed hard, one knee hitting a sharp stone that cut through her apron and frock. She struggled to get up, but the boys closed in around her. She pushed the boy closest to her, only to see Domingo leap through an opening in her sleeve and run frantically toward the square.

"Rat!" screamed a boy, pointing as Domingo raced away. He tugged at Maria's frock, shouting derisively, *"Rat! Rat!"*

"Domingo!" Maria yelled, and her call seemed to surprise the boys. They stepped back in confusion and she seized her chance. She ran after the tiny animal as he headed into the crowd of peddlers and shoppers.

Shrieks arose as Domingo cut a wild and erratic path

through the maze of carts and people, with Maria chasing after him. Her heart beat heavily in her chest and she gasped for breath.

I've been shut up on the ship for so long, I can't keep running. I haven't got the strength. Just at that moment, she saw Domingo pause, standing on his hind legs and sniffing the air. She didn't lose a second. She pulled a chunk of biscuit from her bag and tossed it as close to him as she could. He grabbed it in his mouth and began to run off again, but she had gained a few steps on him. She hurried after him, and again called, "Domingo!" Perhaps he will recognize my voice and stop.

He darted behind the wheel of a low wheelbarrow filled with giant red cabbages, and a stout woman picked up a stiff broom and raised it menacingly.

Maria pushed the woman off-balance and grabbed Domingo, shoving him, biscuit and all, into her sleeve. The woman and her broom went tumbling backward across the cabbages, knocking the wheelbarrow on its side and sending leafy cabbages rolling across the marketplace.

A farmer grabbed Maria's hood and shook her violently while a crowd gathered, yelling and shaking their fists at her. She stopped struggling. I have nowhere to run. Let the crowd do what they will, she thought hopelessly, slumping against the man's grasp. She felt Domingo trembling inside her sleeve.

Two men strode toward the commotion. Each carried a long wooden staff in his hand, which seemed a symbol of their importance. The crowd parted and fell silent.

There was an angry conversation in Dutch, and although Maria could not understand a single word, she knew the woman she had knocked over and the cabbage peddler were blaming her for the damage and repeatedly mentioning the word *rat*. They can do what they like to me, she thought, but they can't have Domingo. If they put me in jail, I'll let him go. At least he'll have a chance to get away.

But the men with the wooden staffs didn't check Maria's sleeve. They scolded her, asking questions she couldn't understand. Their impatience grew, and when she remained silent at their repeated inquiries, they placed a tight grip on her arms and led her through the menacing crowd, past the jeering boys, away from the crush of the marketplace toward a vast stone building that loomed at the edge of the square.

7

An Outstretched Hand

ap, click, click. Tap, click, click.

The irregular rhythm of steps came from behind and distracted Maria's thoughts. She wanted to turn her head to see who was making the sounds, but she was afraid that if she moved in any way the two sheriffs would tighten their hold on her arms.

She tried to concentrate on her own difficulties. The lawmen led her closer to the stone building, and its details became clearer. The rooftop was unfinished, and wooden scaffolding surrounded its dome. Workmen, looking like tiny drones, moved carefully along their perches carrying tools and lumber. The arched arcades along the street were finished, and the windows on the basement level were darkened with iron bars. Her legs felt weak. Would they throw her in prison just for chasing Domingo through the marketplace?

Tap, click, click. Tap, click, click. The mysterious sound behind her quickened and mimicked the irregular beating of her heart. Someone would have to hear her story. She was only searching for her family. But who would understand her?

"*Halt!*" shouted a commanding voice, and the tapping on the cobblestones became louder and faster.

Maria did not understand the Dutch word, but it caught the lawmen's attention immediately. They stopped and turned their heads, but didn't loosen their grip. Maria's arms hurt where the sheriffs' strong hands held her tightly. Domingo hadn't stirred. She hoped he was merely trying to hide and that he wasn't hurt.

A portly man hurried breathlessly toward them. He held a cane that tapped against the stones as he rushed along. Then the man's boots clicked with his rapid footsteps. Maria realized that he wasn't leaning on the cane for support, but that it was only an ornament. The cane was made of thick ebony, topped with a carved silver knob that glittered where the sunlight fell between his fingers.

The man stopped a few feet away, and Maria's captors each gave a short bow in his direction. They didn't smile, but they seemed to know him and awaited his explanation for delaying them.

The man with the cane began questioning them in Dutch, speaking in a calm, confident tone. He was not tall, but he had an imposing presence. His double chin spoke of plentiful meals, and his curling mustache and large bulbous nose gave him a somewhat comical look. He wasn't dressed in as fine a manner as the man with the silk-lined cape who had shooed Maria away last night, but his clothes were well tailored and his leather boots were polished to a shine.

The man stopped talking and looked solemnly into Maria's face. She felt uncomfortable under his scrutiny but didn't turn away. He leaned on his cane, tilting his head as he studied her features. A tapered slatted bas-

ket filled with round, reddish fruit nestled in the crook
of his other arm, and he balanced it deftly as he lifted
a long clay pipe to his lips. He drew a long breath on
the pipe and filled the air with a stream of warm, fragrant smoke. As he lowered his hand, Maria heard the
rustle of stiff paper and saw that he also had a small flat
package tucked under his arm.

"*Portugues?*" the man inquired.

She nodded her head emphatically. The man spoke
Portuguese! She began to talk in a rapid stream, telling
him her name and about her search for her family. But
the man interrupted her, shaking his head. She was
confused.

"*Judea?*" he asked her then. Again, she nodded. She
was Portuguese and she was Jewish. If the man had
guessed this much about her, wasn't he Portuguese
himself?

He turned back to the sheriffs and said something
Maria couldn't understand. The lawmen looked at
each other questioningly, and then one shrugged and
dropped his hold on her. Maria could still feel the pres-
sure where his fingers had been.

The man with the cane stuck his pipe in his mouth
and fumbled in his pockets until he produced a few
small coins. He handed them to the sheriff who still
held her, and then motioned him away gruffly. Without a word, the lawmen turned abruptly and strode
back toward the marketplace.

Maria wondered why the man had bothered to res-
cue her from the sheriffs. He pulled out the package he
had held under his arm and handed it to Maria. She
pulled her sleeve tighter and grasped the package in her
left hand. Next, he gave her the basket of fruit. She

smelled its sweet aroma and felt her mouth water with hunger. She wondered what it tasted like, but knew he wasn't giving it to her to eat. She held the small basket against her body with her free arm.

The man beckoned to her to follow him. Without watching to see if she obeyed, he turned toward one of the side streets and resumed his journey. Tap, click, click. Tap, click, click. Maria looked with bewilderment at his receding figure.

I don't have to go with him. Just because he speaks a word or two of Portuguese doesn't mean he'll help me. I could slip away right now and he could never catch me. But where would I go?

Maria had no reason to trust the stranger, but he apparently expected her to follow him and he had entrusted her with his purchases. She tried to guess what the package contained. The brown paper wrapping crackled as she felt its shape. One section of the string-tied bundle seemed thick and soft, and another seemed to contain wooden sticks, slender and hard. Maria looked up and saw the man disappear around a corner, trailing puffs of blue smoke. She hesitated for a brief moment, and then dashed after him.

She caught up as he came to the end of a short alleyway and emerged into the sunlight onto a quiet street bordering a narrow river lined with shady trees. She stayed several steps behind, but he never once turned to see if she followed.

Maria gazed wonderingly at the houses around her. They were built so close together it seemed there wasn't enough space to fit your finger between them. Most were of dark red brick, rising tall and narrow until their roofs peaked in even-stepped gables. From each high rooftop a thick metal hook dangled. What a strange decoration for a house, she thought. The front door of each house stood at the top of several stone steps lined with a black metal railing. A wide glass window faced the street on the first level, and smaller windows with their shutters thrown open to the warming air graced the second and third stories above.

The man sauntered across a curved bridge, tapping his cane as he went. She looked down into the dark, muddy waters below and smelled the pungent odor of rotting garbage that floated downstream. The streets, however, were immaculate, appearing washed and swept.

Maria began to notice people in a few of the houses, some leaning out of upper windows and arranging fluffy comforters to air on the windowsill. In several of the large front windows, white-capped women occupied with needle and thread sat in tall-backed wooden chairs. A few called a greeting to the mysterious stranger and he raised his pipe in acknowledgment. Then the women saw Maria following and stared at her curiously.

The noise and bustle of the marketplace had been left behind, and Maria felt as if she had entered a new world. A flower vendor set vases along a shady spot near the river and bent over his graceful, colorful blooms, arranging them to their best advantage. Farther on a vegetable seller sat under a large blue umbrella chatting with a woman who had just filled her handbasket with potatoes and squash. They stopped their conversation abruptly as she walked by. The woman stared rudely, and the peddler shook his head in disapproval.

Maria slowed down, wondering again who the man was and where he was taking her. When she heard his familiar tapping stop, she looked ahead to see him turn and give a kindly nod in her direction.

"Drie gracht," he said encouragingly, holding up three fingers and pointing to the water they had just crossed.

He was not speaking Portuguese now. What did the words mean? Was he telling her they must cross three more rivers? He continued steadily on, and she followed. They passed through wide streets and narrow lanes, past ornate houses topped with carved statues, and plain ones with only lacy curtains in their windows for decoration. They walked by a shop where a huge pair of wooden scissors hung as a sign and two tailors worked patiently in the front window.

Domingo poked his head insistently against Maria's sleeve, and she let the wide cuff fall open so he could sniff the smells of Amsterdam and share her amazement at the passing scenes. His nose suddenly twitched expectantly, and he stretched his head toward the fruit basket. If the stranger had offered her some of the fruit, she would gladly have shared it with the curious rat, but she couldn't allow him to nibble what wasn't hers.

"No, no, Domingo," she scolded in a whisper. But her companion couldn't contain his hunger. He stepped cautiously onto the wrapped package she held, trying to scramble across to the tantalizing fruit. She tucked the basket under her arm and placed him back into her sleeve, pulling the cuff tight. The rat gave a squeak of protest and pushed against her wrist, but Maria was satisfied that he couldn't get out. In a few moments, she felt him retreat farther back along her forearm, wiggling about in the loose sleeve of her baggy frock.

"Soon, Domingo," she said soothingly under her breath. "I'll find a place for you soon." She hoped her words were true.

She crossed two more bridges with dark water flowing beneath and flat-bottomed boats laden with barrels and crates rowing past. She began to notice that the course of the water was curiously straight, as straight as a road, and that the banks were lined with smooth stone walls. She had never seen a river that appeared so regular that it did not seem natural.

Maria sensed a peacefulness in this part of the city. She hoped she would never have to go back to the marketplace with its noise and jostling, its wild boys, and frightening rat catcher.

She looked again at the neat houses nestled tightly against each other. My parents could be in any one of these, she thought, and she dared to hope the quiet gentleman just ahead would help her find them. Still, she hadn't gotten over the shock of discovering that Isobel might not have made it to Amsterdam. While Maria searched for her parents, she would also have to find word of the lost ship.

Her thoughts were interrupted as the man paused to speak with a garishly dressed woman who walked in the opposite direction. She hung back as the two spoke a stream of words that had as little meaning for Maria as if she were deaf. The woman eyed Maria distastefully but tried to ignore her while she chattered at the older man. She was dressed unlike any of the women at the marketplace, and nothing like the modestly attired women Maria had seen tending to their homes. The woman was tall and angular and seemed to have painted her face as red as the fabric of her stiff, rustling dress. Her lips fairly glowed with shiny crimson gloss. Her face was powdered a ghostly white and each cheekbone was highlighted with a bright splotch of rosy color. What struck Maria the most, however, was the curly orange hair that seemed to spring in a wild, tousled mass from beneath a silky red hat decorated with long streamers of satin ribbon. The man seemed a bit uncomfortable with the conversation and the woman seemed to be complaining of something in a singsong voice that rose and fell like the whine of a hungry cat.

As Maria tried to take her eyes from the startling figure before her, she felt a light clawing at her arm and looked down to see Domingo pulling himself energetically through a small hole he had gnawed in the coarse sackcloth of her sleeve. He dashed along her arm and up to her shoulder, sniffing his way toward the enticing fruit she held in her other arm.

She turned her back, trying to hide Domingo from the pair in front of her, but she was not quick enough to escape the woman's sharp glance. Her painted face contorted into a horrified grimace and she let out a piercing shriek that brought the entire neighborhood to their windows to see what had caused such distress. The woman sagged into a mock swoon and the gentleman caught her as she collapsed. His ebony cane clattered against the cobblestones and his clay pipe shattered against the woman's sharp elbow.

As for Domingo, he had never heard such a frightening noise. He retreated behind Maria's neck, seeking refuge in the tangle of her long hair. She groped for

him, but with the packages in her arms and Domingo's
entanglement, she couldn't reach him at all.

The woman recovered her senses somewhat and
staggered to her feet, pushing the man away from her
and babbling in horrified tones. Maria was now very
familiar with one Dutch word, and that was *"Rat!"*
The woman swayed unsteadily for a moment and then
hurried away in the direction of the marketplace, her
hand against her powdered throat, her skirt rustling,
and her delicate pointed shoes mincing along the cobblestones in a shuffling clatter.

The man bent to retrieve his cane and looked from
the shattered bowl of his pipe to Maria's face. She felt
Domingo peering from behind the curtain of her hair
and she was about to flee the man's wrath when he
suddenly burst into a deep, bellowing laugh. He
pointed at Domingo with his cane and held his ample
belly as if he would burst. He tossed his broken pipe
carelessly to the gutter and reached for her arm, pulling her onward without even glancing back at the car-
rot-haired woman who had fled.

"Charmant!" he exclaimed, chuckling, and although Maria had no idea what he said, she felt his
amusement, and even his approval of Domingo's antics. She glanced from the hole in her sleeve to her
shoulder where Domingo peered curiously from between her strands of hair.

Abruptly the man stopped in his tracks as if he had
suddenly remembered something important. He
looked at Maria and at Domingo. Then he scratched
at the straggling gray hair that poked out at the front
of his hat. Almost immediately, his face brightened
and he let out a satisfied "Aha!"

He took the basket of fruit from Maria and emptied
it, placing each piece on a set of house steps nearby.
Then he slid the small package from under Maria's
arm, untied the string that fastened it closed, and laid
its contents alongside. Maria saw a bundle of stiff white
fabric and four long-handled wooden brushes. Was this
what had brought the man to market so early this
morning?

He took the empty wooden basket and motioned to
Maria to put the rat inside. Maria tried out her newest
word. *"Rat?"* The man nodded approvingly at her
quick understanding.

She reached for the furry creature and held him
gently in her hands. He immediately lay back contentedly and began licking his pink tongue against her fingers. The man chuckled with pleasure.

"Domingo," she said, introducing her companion to
the man.

"Ah, Domingo," repeated the man. Gingerly, he
reached a stout finger toward the animal and when he
sensed no danger he rubbed its furry head with obvious
delight. Then he motioned to the basket. Maria placed
Domingo carefully inside and instead of becoming
frightened by its confines, he seemed reassured by its
protection. The man picked up a piece of fruit and bit
off a chunk. There was juicy white pulp under the rosy
peel. He handed the morsel to Domingo, who held it
in his paws and began chewing greedily. The man
smiled, and as Domingo ate he ripped a square of stiff
fabric from the cloth he had purchased and used the
string from the package to fasten it onto the top of the
basket. Domingo was snug inside his wooden cage.

The man admired his handiwork. Then he stuck his

brushes into a pocket and began stuffing the fruit in as well. Maria showed him her apron sack and the man handed her some, too.

"*Appel,*" he explained as she dropped them in.

When they had gathered up all the items and Domingo's new home, he began walking again, munching on the apple he had shared with Domingo. He pulled another from his bulging pocket and offered it to Maria. She held the fruit to her nose, savoring its crisp, sweet smell, and then took a bite, holding the stem ends as she had seen the man do. Its tart sweetness filled her mouth. She couldn't remember the last time she had tasted anything so satisfying.

Domingo poked his snout comically between two wooden slats, his paws grasping their edges like a prisoner in jail. Maria pushed a piece of apple through the cage into his waiting mouth and walked along, close on the heels of her new acquaintance. Any man who could accept Domingo must have kindness in him.

When the next bridge was crossed, she saw that it spanned a broad swiftly flowing river that reflected the blue sky overhead. This was the third river, she thought, and her anticipation grew. Their walk from the marketplace must be nearing an end.

The man turned and pointed to a fine, wide house, bigger than any Maria had seen that morning. It was twice as wide as the narrow homes they had passed before, with four windows in a row facing the street on the two upper levels and bright red shutters thrust open to the sunlight.

"*Breestraat,*" the man said, gesturing to the street on which they stood. "*Comen,*" he coaxed her as he climbed the steps to the heavy wooden door that led inside.

Maria gazed at the thick, varnished door as he opened it for her, and her hand grazed the rough white stone that framed it. The top of the door was decorated with an ornate wooden triangle, and a carved gable adorned the crest of the roof. From the peak, the same gray metal hook that she had seen on every Amsterdam house dangled mysteriously.

"Hendrickje!" called the man as he stepped into the doorway. "Hendrickje!"

She hesitated at the entryway, peering into a large black-and-white tiled foyer. Its walls were hung with paintings, huge framed paintings that reached all the way to the ceiling. Her eyes widened.

The man gestured toward the foyer. Maria pressed Domingo's basket closer to her chest and stepped in.

8

Easels in the Attic

ight footsteps approached from the rear of the house and the man who had guided Maria from the marketplace reached for the basket that held Domingo. He slid the wooden cage under an elegant tapestry-covered bench in the entryway and stepped in front of it. Maria was left standing awkwardly with an apple core in one hand and lumpy bulges protruding from her apron sack. She clasped her hands behind her back, hiding the remains of the chewed fruit.

A small, pink-cheeked woman entered the foyer, her soft leather shoes gliding across the smooth black-and-white tiles. She approached with a warm smile and eyed Maria without surprise. She stood no higher than the man's prominent nose but looked up at him with assurance.

She asked him a question, and an expression of concern came over her face as she listened to the answer. She studied the visitor more closely and Maria tried to meet her cool, steady gaze without shame. The woman's full reddish brown hair was brushed carefully behind her ears and held neatly in place with pearl-studded combs. She wore a deep blue cotton skirt with a matching jacket that reached down to her hips. She was plump around the middle, but her oval face was slender and youthful.

Maria observed that the woman seemed much younger than the man, but she felt they must be husband and wife, simply from the familiar way they looked at each other. There was a clatter of dishes in the back room and the sound of water splashing in a tin pan. Maria guessed there must be at least one servant. In such a large house, she guessed the family would need many. Perhaps that's why the man brought me, she thought. I'm willing to work, but only if I can still search for my family.

"Hendrickje," the man announced, gesturing toward his wife.

Maria flattened the apple core against her palm and gave a short bow in the woman's direction. "Maria Ben Lazar," she said, introducing herself.

Hendrickje smiled and then turned toward her husband. "Heer van Rijn," she said. Maria sensed a formality in this introduction but did not understand the words. The Dutch language was so difficult to her ears. It seemed the woman was to be called "Hendreeka," but she was not sure what the man's name was. "Hare-von-rine," she repeated to herself. Was that his name or was it a title?

The man gave some instructions to his wife, who nodded in agreement and walked toward the open front door. She stepped out and the morning sun lit a few stray wisps of hair with an orange glow. Without a word, she closed the door behind her. Her leather

shoes brushed softly against the stone walk until the
sound faded into the distance.

Maria's host let out a wild chuckle, as if he were
about to embark on a delightful adventure. She was
startled by his deep, guttural laugh and looked at him
uneasily.

The man placed his cane in a tall vase that held
three other walking sticks, and retrieved Domingo's
basket. He tucked it under one arm and pulled Maria
by the wrist toward the broad staircase that overlooked
the entryway. Her thick sandals clattered noisily across
the tiles and up the polished wooden stairs. The staircase and upper landing opened over the great foyer,
and she couldn't take her eyes from the dark, imposing
paintings that hung on the white plaster walls. Light
reflected off thick paint that nearly rose from the canvas, as if begging to be touched as well as seen. She
was mesmerized by their images and for a moment felt
that she, too, was a painting, suspended in time and
space, gazing helplessly on a rich man's mansion.

The man pulled her along, stopped abruptly at the
end of the second-floor landing, and thrust Domingo's
basket into her arms. As she grasped it, he noticed that
she still held the apple core between her thumb and
forefinger. He took it and tossed it carelessly out the
open widow. Maria watched it sail noiselessly between
the house in which she was standing and the neighbor's house, which was so close that she couldn't believe there was any space for an apple core, or even a
pigeon feather. The orange tiled roof of the adjacent
building was so near that she could touch it without so
much as leaning from the window.

Domingo had smelled the apple core and pressed to

the edge of the basket. He grasped the slats with his tiny pink fingers and wrinkled his nose through the space between.

But Maria had no time to indulge him. She stood in bewilderment as the man dashed into a large front room and clumsily unloaded his pockets of apples, paintbrushes, and cloth, dropping them onto a cluttered table near the doorway. She peered into the darkened room. It was a jumble of plaster statues, and disembodied models of arms and legs and hands. Heavy tapestry cloths were piled in heaps, and several tall woven baskets were filled with spears, bows, arrows, flutes, feathery plumes, and dried plants. Maria saw elegant Chinese bowls filled with colorful stones and gracefully shaped seashells like those she remembered decorating her parents' home in Portugal.

In a fleeting memory, she could almost see her father examining a perfect conch shell at the marketplace, showing her its lustrous pink underside, and haggling with the vendor over the price. That shell had rested on a table near her bedroom window until she had left it so suddenly the night she was kidnapped.

She wondered what had happened to that perfect pink shell, but the man had already returned and led her toward a narrow door that opened onto the hall. She took one last look behind her and saw the shadowy shape of a tall wooden easel set boldly in the middle of the confusing room, surrounded by unframed paintings stacked against the walls.

There was no time to wonder what the room was used for. The man clomped noisily up a narrow, nearly perpendicular staircase. As they approached the top he cleared his throat with a loud "Harumph!" Sounds of shuffling footsteps and the din of competing conversations from above suddenly fell silent. Maria emerged into the sudden light of a broad attic. Along one wall she saw a row of cots separated into narrow cubicles by sheets of stiff canvas nailed into the open rafters above. At the foot of each bed a heavy trunk rested on the rough plank floor.

The cubicles were small and unobtrusive, and the sunny attic was dominated by a cluster of easels set haphazardly near the center of the room. At each easel, a young man holding a stub of charcoal sketched on a large sheet of white paper.

The man slammed a door at the top of the stairs. Maria moved closer to one of the open windows, setting Domingo's basket in the shade on the floor beside her. She tried to avoid the curious eyes that stared boldly, even as the young men stood still at their easels and murmured respectful greetings to the older man as he strode into their midst. He made an announcement and the attentive group immediately placed fresh white paper onto their easels. As they stood expectantly, the man seemed to relate a story, speaking in a quiet narrative that contrasted with his opening words. He paused and beckoned to Maria with an outstretched hand.

She hung back. Her face flushed with embarrassment as the young men turned in her direction. The man came toward her, speaking soothingly. He took her hand and led her forward, speaking softly all the while. He stopped in the center of the floor and took a piece of charcoal from a nearby table laden with pots of black and red ink and littered with long-handled pens. He picked up a scrap of paper and smoothed it against the wall. With just a few quick movements, he drew several lines and handed it to her. She looked with amazement at the picture. It was a sketch of her, capturing her feelings of fear and embarrassment, along with the wild look of her hair. It was not just a drawing of Maria, it was her very essence.

The man gestured to the young men poised at their easels with the chalk between their fingers. Now she understood.

This must be a school for artists, and the man who saved me from the sheriffs this morning has to be their teacher. She wondered if he had done all the paintings and drawings that adorned the walls of the house, for certainly the cluttered room on the floor below must be his own studio. He drew her image so effortlessly he had to be a master.

He's brought me from the marketplace so that his pupils can draw me. Remembering her dirty, ill-fitting frock and her bare feet showing through the open sandals, Maria felt deeply ashamed. She dropped her eyes to the floor and shook her head to refuse the master's plan.

But his intentions were not to be ignored. He lifted her chin with his thick fingers and tilted her head slightly so that she seemed to be looking behind her. Then he held up the palms of his hands, indicating that he did not want her to move. He removed the apples from her apron pocket and arranged her frock so that the fabric was nearly taut against the front of her legs. The thick folds of the brown sackcloth trailed behind her. Maria felt trapped. She was afraid to move and too self-conscious to stand still.

"Ah!" said the man, interrupting the uncomfortable

silence around her. He removed the cover from Domingo's basket. The rat immediately poked his head
curiously over the top. There was a nervous gasp
among some of the students and then a few suppressed
chuckles. Maria reached for him, relieved to have his
familiar company in the midst of her confusion. He
responded at once to her touch, nuzzling her hands as
she patted the sleek fur on his head.

"So, little friend," she whispered, "you've come to
keep me company again."

There was a murmur of amazement from the art students as the master cut a large chunk of apple and
placed it enticingly on Maria's shoulder. As Domingo
scrambled after it, he gestured to her not to move.

Once again he turned her face slightly toward the
shoulder where Domingo sat. He tugged at the hood of
her frock, arranged her hair loosely across it, and
placed her arms at a slightly bent angle in front of her.
She imagined that she looked as if she were running
from something, with Domingo riding along on her
shoulder for protection.

Now the students leaned into their work, studying
her with professional curiosity and sketching, rubbing,
and changing their drawings. Maria felt as if she were
once again escaping from the friars in Recife. She remembered the heat of the tropical morning when she
and Isobel had hurried through the thick brush at the
edge of the path to make their way unnoticed toward
the docks and the waiting ships. Her thoughts wandered until she lost all awareness of her surroundings.

The sound of a church bell striking in the distance
roused her from her memories. How many times had it
sounded? Was it still morning? The raw dampness of

the dawn had been replaced by a rising heat, and Maria's frock clung to her damp skin. She felt as if days had gone by since she had searched the marketplace for Isobel, but it had only been a few short hours.

The students were absorbed in their work and she was now merely an object to be copied, not a disheveled young woman who badly needed a bath and clean clothes. Even the master was drawing, sitting on a low stool that seemed much too small for his portly body. He balanced a sheet of paper on a flat board, which he had placed upon his lap. His eyes reflected total concentration and a frown creased his forehead, but he also had a look of contentment. He reminded Maria of the friars in the monastery when they prayed. Their faces wore an expression of physical strain mixed with pure joy.

Domingo explored Maria's shoulders for a while, pulling playfully at her hair, and then walked carefully along her outstretched arm until he dropped into her sleeve and curled up to sleep. She also felt as if she needed to sleep. Her arms were tired from holding them out so long and her eyes had grown weary of focusing on the blank wall opposite her gaze. She tried to let her imagination wander again, but this time she could not stop thinking about where she was and what she would do next. She heard the church bells ring ten o'clock.

The master set his sketch aside and began to walk among his pupils, stopping at each easel, studying the drawing and speaking quietly to each young artist. Occasionally he took his own chalk and penciled in a few lines or erased a mark that was not to his liking. By his tone of voice, Maria sensed that he was not harsh in his judgments but encouraging.

As he made his rounds, there was a meek knocking on the attic door.

"*Weggaan!*" he shouted, so roughly that Maria nearly lost her balance. Domingo, too, gave a start, and poked his head nervously through the hole he had chewed in her sleeve.

The knock sounded again, not loudly, but insistently. The master stomped to the door and shouted a question through it. A timid voice answered in pleading tones, mixed now and then with a nervous sigh. He angrily threw his chalk against the wall, where it left a jagged black line before falling to the floor.

He walked directly to Maria and patted her on the shoulder. She felt that she could now lower her arms and relax from her unnatural pose. The students began shuffling at their easels, talking among themselves and examining one another's work. She couldn't see their drawings and was curious. Did they draw her wretched and dirty, or did they see past her appearance as the master had?

He brought Domingo's basket to her, and she dropped the sleepy animal back into his cage and fastened the covering over the top. With a few words to his students, he then led her to a door at the rear of the attic that she hadn't noticed before. It opened to an outside stairway. She followed the master down the back of the house and past a small flower garden blooming with pink, yellow, and purple blossoms. Their brightness contrasted with the somber colors inside the house, and with the spare dark and light shadows of the attic studio. She breathed in the fragrance

of the air, so different from the smells that had as-
saulted her in the marketplace and along the rivers.

The man walked to a small wooden shed and unlatched the door. A tall window cast its sunlit shadow
across tools, flowerpots, a rusty spade, and a splintery
wooden wheelbarrow that lay upside down in a corner.
The master placed Domingo's cage on the dirt floor
inside. He gestured toward the house and said, "Hendrickje," shaking his head in disapproval. Maria understood. No housewife would tolerate a rat in her
kitchen, and the shed seemed a fine place for Domingo. She took a saucer from under an empty flowerpot and filled it with the last of the contents of her
water bottle. The master loosened the canvas from
Domingo's cage and closed the shed door tightly.

Maria smiled and "Hare-von-rine" almost smiled
back. He tried to act gruff, she thought, but he seemed
a kind and understanding man.

With more confidence than she had felt in weeks,
Maria followed the man into a neat kitchen just off the
garden. Hendrickje was there with a servant girl and a
tub of steaming water set in a sunny niche. Hendrickje
shooed the master back outdoors and handed Maria
two lavish gifts before she followed him out. They were
a thick cake of soap and a soft cotton towel.

9

Conversations in the Parlor

he scent of lavender surrounded Maria and permeated her dreams. She nestled deeper into her bed as she watched her mother reach for the conch shell on the bedside table. The woman moved slowly and her head was covered by a lacy scarf that cast a dark shadow across her face. Maria could not see her features, but she knew it was her mother. She reached out from under her covers to take the shell her mother held out to her, but before she could touch its shiny pink underside or listen to the ocean sounds that rose mysteriously from its depths, other sounds interrupted her vision. Quiet conversations persisted in the background, and a pot clattered noisily to the floor.

Maria pushed deeper into the feather pillow, trying to hold on to the dream before it faded. Caught between the world of sleeping and waking she reached for the shell, knowing she couldn't touch it. Her hand banged against the wooden frame that enclosed her bed and she awoke.

She was not in her bed in Portugal, as she had dreamed. Maria breathed deeply the faint fragrance of lavender that arose from the linens. Her mother had always placed a sprig of dried lavender between the sheets and, although Maria was in a different bed, the smell alone had made her feel that she was safely tucked into her own bed in Lisbon.

She dangled her feet over the edge of the high bed before letting them slip down onto the cool tiled floor. She smoothed the sheets and coverlet, replaced the lavender sprig between them, and pulled the blue curtain across the frame. It was as if the bed no longer existed.

Maria still marveled at the bed cupboard Hendrickje had revealed to her after her bath. A feathery mattress rested in a niche carved neatly into the wall of the back parlor. With the curtain open, Maria had curled up in the bed, feeling the luxury of sheets and a pillow. Now that the curtain was closed again, the bed seemed to disappear and the room turned back into a parlor ready for guests.

The wine-colored dress and small linen cap that Hendrickje had given her were draped neatly over the arm of a chair, and Maria slipped into the soft fabric, fumbling at the tiny cloth buttons that fastened it down the front. She pulled on the dark cotton stockings and thin-soled shoes, her toes pinching against the tips. She couldn't remember when she had worn anything other than a pair of thick leather sandals on her bare feet.

How long have I slept? Maria glanced around the room and saw the sun shining through a slit between the curtains and casting an angular beam across the floor. Hendrickje had insisted she rest after her bath, and Maria had been too tired to resist. If it was still

afternoon, then she hadn't slept long, yet she felt re-
freshed and alert.

A ceramic bowl filled with water stood on a tall table
below a looking glass. A towel and a hairbrush had
been laid out beside the basin. Maria washed and stood
before the mirror, brushing her hair. She felt gloriously
clean after so many weeks shut up on the ship.

She had nearly cried out when the house servant
pulled the comb through her tangled hair, and feared
there was no way of brushing it out without cutting the
knots. But one by one, the matted clumps had finally
yielded. Now as she brushed, her shiny hair fell loosely
around her shoulders. Maria thought longingly of her
silver hair combs. How she would love to hold her hair
back with their filigreed design.

But she had given those combs to Isobel. If her ship
makes it to a distant port those combs might buy her
passage to Amsterdam. I'd willingly give them up forever if it meant finding Isobel again. Maria picked up
the simple white linen cap and pinned it on her head.

Now Maria followed the sound of talking toward the
kitchen. Hendrickje smiled a greeting. "Ah, Maria!
Goedemorgen."

The girl who had helped Maria with her bath did
not smile. She looked at Maria and muttered, "Goe-
demiddag."

Maria was confused again. She didn't know how to
reply. Hendrickje poured her a mug of tea and motioned to her to sit down. A long oak table, as big as
any at the monastery, was placed along one wall in the
kitchen, and mismatched chairs were neatly pushed
around it. Maria sat down and sipped her tea, and hungrily ate some dry toast that the girl set before her.

"*Mijn naam is Freeda,*" said the girl, pointing to herself. "Freeda."

Maria tried to repeat her words. "Mine nam ees Maria."

Hendrickje clapped her hands with approval. Then
she turned back to the high wooden worktable where
she and Freeda were busily chopping fish into a bowl.
Maria quickly finished her tea and cleared her dishes.
As she looked out the window into the yard, it seemed
that almost no time had gone by since her bath. But
there was no sign of the metal tub in the kitchen. How
long had she been asleep?

Hendrickje seemed to understand her unspoken
question. She waved her finger in a small circle. Then
Maria understood. She had slept an entire day. It was
noontime, but it was the day after she had arrived. If
Hendrickje had wished her good morning when she entered the kitchen, perhaps Freeda had wished her good
evening! She glanced at the shed. Poor Domingo
hadn't been given food or water since she left him yesterday, but she didn't dare let Hendrickje or Freeda
know he was there. She hoped he could wait a little
longer until she could take care of him.

Freeda set a large market basket filled with fruit on
the table, and pushed a large bowl into Maria's arms.
She motioned to the fruit and gave out some instructions Maria couldn't understand. But it was clear she
wanted the fruit placed in the bowl. Maria was happy
to help. She began separating the fruit onto the table
as a knock sounded at the front door. Hendrickje left
the room, and in a moment Maria heard laughter and
greetings in the hallway. The sound of conversation
moved closer until Maria heard the guests being ush-

ered into the parlor where she had been sleeping. Apparently, the master and Hendrickje were having guests for lunch.

A small brown bee darted from a cluster of purple grapes, startling Maria. It buzzed menacingly close to her face and then landed on a fragrant orange. After a moment of inspection, the bee realized the orange had neither pollen nor nectar to offer. It flew off through the window, announcing its disappointment with a vibrating buzz that soon trailed off into silence. Maria envied the insect and its freedom. At least a bee always knows where home is, she thought.

She turned her attention back to the fruit she was arranging, placing it into the glazed Chinese bowl at random. Freeda looked over at Maria's handiwork and clucked her tongue in disapproval. She strode over to the table, dumped the fruit out in a jumbled heap, and gestured how she wanted it arranged.

Freeda was a plump, pockmarked young woman who did not look much older than Maria. She had bumbled about the kitchen yesterday, dropping the soap and spilling as much hot water on the floor as she managed to pour into Maria's bath. She shuffled about with her head down and seemed almost frightened of Hendrickje but was now boldly giving Maria orders.

She wants me to believe she is in charge. I suppose she thinks I'm stupid because I don't speak Dutch, but I have nothing to prove to her. I'm here by my own choice, and I'll gladly help out, but I'm done with silently following orders.

She draped the last bunch of grapes at the top of the fruit bowl while Freeda prepared a platter of sliced cheese and bread and a concoction of pungent chopped fish with fresh onions, piled on a nest of leafy greens.

"*Haring salade,*" the girl said, but to Maria it was just chopped fish. She studied her fruit arrangement. The friars at the monastery wouldn't have approved of anything so artistic, nor would they have provided more than a rough wooden bowl for their table. I'll have to learn new ways if I stay in the master's kitchen. But of course, I don't plan to be here long.

Freeda scowled at the finished fruit bowl and snatched the top cluster of grapes from its perch, rearranging it with a mutter of annoyance. Apparently the girl felt she must have final authority over the arrangement. She handed the bowl back and impatiently motioned Maria toward the back parlor.

Maria realized she was expected to serve the fruit to the guests. She paled at the thought of walking into a roomful of strangers.

"*Doorgaan!*" Freeda barked, giving her a shove toward the door. Maria pointedly put the grapes back the way she wanted them and glared at the girl. Then she straightened up and headed toward the sound of quiet conversation that was harder to decipher than the humming of the bee.

She slipped into the room, her smooth soles tapping softly on the tiled floor. The drapes had been tied back and the window opened and the room was bright and airy. Paintings festooned the walls, like every room Maria had seen in the house, and the lifelike portraits made her feel as if a second group of strangers watched her every move. The same sky blue fabric that closed off the bed cupboard covered the elegant chairs on which the guests sat.

Freeda entered behind Maria and set out platters of food on a lace-covered mahogany table against the back wall. Maria set the fruit bowl down and followed the girl out, returning with an armful of plates, napkins, and silverware. She stood by as the master and Hendrickje and the smiling couple who visited them filled their plates with food and sat down to eat, balancing their plates on their laps. Freeda brought in a tray of wine and sparkling goblets. After filling a glass for each person, she set a decanter of red wine on the table and sidled back to the kitchen.

The conversation continued between mouthfuls, and as Maria turned toward the kitchen, she heard her own name mentioned. They know I can't understand them and they talk about me as if I weren't here. The master called to her as she stepped out the doorway. He gestured with his wineglass to the man seated on the chair beside him and said, "Rabbi Menasseh Ben Israel. *Portugues.*"

She caught her breath. If the man was Portuguese, surely he would know where to find her parents. Had the master sent Hendrickje out yesterday to invite this couple to their house to help her? The rabbi spoke soothingly, his coarse gray beard moving with every word.

"Come sit here by me." He indicated a soft blue cushioned chair near the window. She sat anxiously on the edge of the chair, grateful for the breeze that brushed across her warm face. "What has brought you to Amsterdam, all alone?"

"I don't know where to begin," she faltered.

"You are from Portugal, or Brazil?" the Rabbi prodded her.

"I lived with my parents in Lisbon," she said. "We were *conversos*, but our family was always under the king's protection." The rabbi nodded encouragingly. "Then one night I overheard my parents talking. Father said we were in danger and told my mother he was making arrangements for all of us to go to Amsterdam. But a few nights later, while my father was away, the soldiers came . . . soldiers of the Inquisition."

The rabbi stroked his short beard with his thumb and forefinger. "How long ago was that?"

Maria admitted that she didn't know the year she had been kidnapped. "I was only ten," she explained. "But it has been six years since then. I'm certain of that."

Rabbi Ben Israel sighed. "I know the date well, child. It was 1648, when the leaders of the Inquisition persuaded the king that the children of *conversos* must be taken from their parents to be certain they were not secretly being taught the Jewish faith." He shook his head sadly. "So many of our children were lost."

He turned to the master and his wife and spoke briefly in Dutch. The master lifted his eyebrows in surprise but said nothing. Hendrickje showed no response at all but quietly got up and passed the platter of food around. Only her husband helped himself to another portion. He then held out his empty wineglass and Hendrickje calmly replaced the platter, refilled the wineglasses, and collected the empty plates. Maria thought she should be helping and began to get up from the chair.

"Please continue," said the rabbi's wife. Maria hadn't paid much notice to the tiny woman before now. She was so slight and quiet that she seemed to

fade into the chair as if she weren't there. Her gray hair
was piled atop her head in a neat bun, and a white lace
cap was fastened under her chin. She wore a pale blue
dress trimmed at the neck and sleeves with soft lace,
and sat with her smooth, olive-skinned hands folded
in her lap. Her dark, heavy-lidded eyes reminded Maria
of her mother.

"The soldiers took my sister and me and sent us
across the ocean to a monastery in Brazil. Isobel was
only six then." She paused while the rabbi again translated for the others.

"Many of the other children died," she said. "There
was so much work and so little food. They made us
learn their prayers, but we only spoke them with our
mouths, never with our hearts. And always, always, I
thought of escape, some way for us to find our parents
again."

She noticed the master was barely listening. He had
set his empty plate on the floor beside him, taken a
piece of paper and a stub of charcoal from his pocket,
and was absorbed in drawing. He seemed to have been
transported to another world, away from the back parlor and the people who surrounded him.

"And how did you escape, finally?" prodded the
rabbi.

"It was because of the battle in Recife," Maria said.
"When the Portuguese army defeated the Dutch, they
took over the governing of the colony. Two of the friars
from our monastery planned to establish a branch of
the Inquisition in Recife. I knew that if Isobel and I
could travel out of the forest, there was a better chance
for escape. I told one of the friars that my sister and I

would be willing to help them with their work, and he decided to bring us."

"You're a clever girl," the rabbi's wife complimented her, while her husband again translated into Dutch.

"The great exodus from Recife is well known here," the rabbi said. "This year of 1654 has seen a flood of colonists forced to escape from Portuguese rule. Many are Jews. But how did you get away from Recife? You must have been closely watched."

"The night before our escape, the friars sent us to sleep alone in a barn. I was able to tell Isobel my plan to mix in with the colonists who were sailing for Amsterdam. I was sure we could hide on those boats."

Her shoulders slumped. "I had to separate from Isobel," she whispered. She lifted her face questioningly to the rabbi. "How could we both stow away on one small ship?" He touched her arm and said simply, "I understand."

"I was certain we'd both land in Amsterdam together," Maria explained, "but I can't find her. Perhaps she's on the lost ship that I heard about at the dock. Or maybe she never got away at all." She voiced the thought she hadn't yet dared to admit. "Maybe the friars caught her."

Tears filled her eyes and the room blurred into a blue haze. "How will I tell my parents I've lost Isobel?"

Her words hung in the air. The rabbi cleared his throat and his wife dabbed her lace cuff at the corners of her eyes. "Let us find your parents first," the rabbi said gently, "then we'll see about Isobel. We have some connections, we Portuguese Jews. We have ways of bringing back our own."

Maria straightened up and wiped at her wet cheeks.

"I almost forgot the most important part. My father is Abraham Ben Lazar. Surely you know him."

The rabbi and his wife looked at each other with surprise. They conversed for a moment in Dutch, and both Hendrickje and the master joined in the brief exchange. Then he turned to Maria. "Did you say Ben Lazar? The king's adviser? Why, of course I know the name, but I wasn't aware that he was in Amsterdam."

Maria felt as if she had been slapped. First Isobel gone, and now her parents. She looked at the rabbi in stunned silence, and he immediately seemed to regret his bluntness.

"Of course, Rabbi Menasseh could be mistaken," his wife said.

"There are nearly two thousand of us here in the city," he interjected quickly, "and not everyone is in contact with me. But a man such as Ben Lazar should be known. First I'll ask Dr. Bonus. If your mother or father has needed the advice of a physician any time these past six years, surely they have seen Dr. Ephraim Bonus."

Maria stood up. "But where will I go?" she asked. "In the marketplace, they were going to put me in jail. I thought I'd find my family as soon as I could find someone in the Portuguese community. I didn't think I would be here alone."

"You're not alone," offered the rabbi's wife. Her long, tapered fingers fluttered delicately in the air as she spoke. "Rembrandt has offered to keep you here, or we can find you a Jewish family, if you would prefer."

"Rembrandt?" asked Maria.

The master put his sketch down and looked up absently. "Eh?" The others laughed.

"Don't you know where you are, child?" The rabbi smiled. "Well, of course, how could you? You've been away from the world too long. You are in the home of Rembrandt van Rijn, probably the greatest artist in the world. You've been here at least a day. Hasn't he sketched you yet?"

His wife laughed, a soft, musical laugh, and translated for Hendrickje and the master. Hendrickje smiled knowingly, and the master merely held out his glass, which was again empty.

"But I don't understand," Maria protested. "I thought his name was Harevonrine."

Now even the master smiled, understanding the confusion.

"*Heer* is the Dutch word for 'gentleman,' " Rabbi Menasseh explained. "Van Rijn is the last name. His first name is Rembrandt, and that's what all the world calls him. Eh, Rembrandt?" He nudged his friend's arm and got an embarrassed grunt in response.

"If you'd like to stay," the rabbi's wife explained, "Rembrandt would like you to pose for him and help out occasionally with the housework. You see, Hendrickje is with child and she needs as much rest as possible." Of course, Maria realized. That was why she looked rather heavy about the middle.

"They can't afford to pay you," the rabbi said, "but you'll be safe here and in the heart of the Jewish quarter. Our friend Rembrandt says he is happiest living among us because he sees the Bible in our faces. I think it's simply because we save him from having to deal with the social graces of Amsterdam society!"

Maria had to decide quickly if she wanted to stay where she was or have the rabbi find another family to

take her in. She didn't want charity. She would rather
work for her keep and she could be useful here. Freeda
removed the food platters from the table, and returned
for the plates, carefully avoiding the one Rembrandt
had set on the floor.

The master's acceptance of Domingo flashed
through Maria's thoughts. If she moved, it wasn't likely
anyone else would willingly accept a small brown and
white rat.

"I'd like to stay," she offered, "and of course, it will
only be for a little while, until I find my parents."

"Yes, yes," the rabbi said thoughtfully, stroking his
beard.

"But I don't speak Dutch," she worried.

"We all had to learn when we first arrived," said the
rabbi's wife. "It's not as difficult as you think. And Titus will be home from school shortly."

"That's Rembrandt's son," explained the rabbi. "You
must have slept through the time he was at home yesterday. In fact, Titus must be about your age. Fourteen
now, I think. I've been teaching him to speak Portuguese since he was a baby, so he'll be a perfect trans-
lator. I'd be willing to bet he'll have you speaking
Dutch in no time. And we're just across the Breestraat,
you know. Why, from the front steps, you could hit
our house with a piece of Rembrandt's chalk."

Maria thanked the rabbi and his wife for their help,
but she wondered if they really could do anything to
find her family. They might ask other members of the
community, but would that be enough? And they had
said nothing about Isobel.

She had expected to stay in Rembrandt's house only

for a day or two, but now she had to face the possibility that this would be her home for weeks, maybe months.

She returned to the kitchen, startling Freeda, who stood at the door talking in hushed tones to a gaunt young man with dark, narrow eyes and thick blond hair. They both looked up guiltily, and then Freeda's visitor pulled his cap over his eyes and hurried away without a word.

The serving girl gruffly offered her a plate of bread, cheese, and herring, first wiping a piece of bread across the mound of chopped fish and biting off a large mouthful. It had been days since Maria had eaten a real meal, but now her appetite was gone and the emptiness in her stomach did not seem to be from lack of food.

Still, she took a bunch of grapes and a few slices of cheese and bread and then walked out of the kitchen to the shed.

10

View from the Shed

omingo snatched the plump grape Maria offered and hopped back to the shelter of his basket. She sat in the partially open doorway of the shed, making sure he couldn't run out. Even at the height of the afternoon, the sun felt welcome and the air was fresh. It was nothing like the oppressive thickness of the Brazilian heat.

Maria looked upward to a patch of blue sky. The yard behind the master's house was a small breath of open space in a landscape crowded with buildings. Rooftops loomed overhead in every direction, and she felt closed in. Even with the confines of the monastery, there had been open sky above and an endless forest around her.

"I see you've made yourself comfortable in your new home," she said softly to Domingo, trying to move her thoughts away from her own sense of isolation. His sleek head turned in her direction, but Domingo kept nibbling on the grape, turning it evenly in his paws and licking the juice when it began to drip. "We're going to live here for a while," she announced, more to herself than to the rat. "But it's just until Rabbi Menasseh helps us find our family. It won't be long."

A heaviness settled over her and she slumped against the doorjamb. Rough splinters poked against her back, but she didn't have enough energy to move away.

Domingo finished the last morsel and then carefully cleaned his paws and face. When he was satisfied with his washing, he bounded toward her, hopping first onto his front paws and then springing his back feet forward in a game of catch-up. He paused and sniffed the folds of her dress suspiciously.

"Do I smell different?" she asked him. "It's about time, don't you think? Now you know what a clean Maria smells like. I'll bet the boys in the market wouldn't throw stones at me now."

She reached out and scratched behind Domingo's delicate ears. At least one thing in her world hadn't changed overnight.

The rat scrambled up her outstretched arm and perched on her shoulder, nuzzling her cheek. When she turned her face toward him, Domingo's rough pink tongue darted out and flicked against her lips. Without thinking, she pulled back with distaste. A tingling sensation lingered on her lips and in spite of her first startled reaction, a warm feeling began to engulf her.

He had kissed her. And why, she asked herself, should a rat be any less affectionate than a cat or a puppy? She held him against her cheek until he squirmed to be set free. "I love you, too, little friend," she whispered.

He suddenly stopped squirming and froze. His ears were pointed alertly, sensing the air. Then Maria heard a sound. A crisp rustling grew louder, like the wind in an approaching storm. Domingo dived under the folds of her dress.

The sound struck a familiar note. She heard the swishing of silky cloth combine with a patter of footsteps. She shrunk into the shadows and held Domingo safely beneath her hand. As she looked toward the house, the noise materialized into the figure of the Lady in Red. It was the same woman who had nearly fainted in Rembrandt's arms yesterday when Domingo made his sudden appearance from the hole in her sleeve. The woman stopped at the foot of the back stairs leading to the attic studio and removed her clicking shoes before climbing up. Her red clothes and hat stood out brightly against the faded brown stairway.

If the woman was calling on the master, why didn't she just knock at the front door? She paused on the landing and looked around as if to be sure she wasn't seen. Then she tossed her red-hatted head and slipped in at the studio door.

Maria sat quite still for a few moments, looking up at the master's studio, but the door remained closed. There is probably nothing at all mysterious about the Lady in Red, she told herself. Perhaps she has dressed up so brightly to have the apprentices paint her. But she remembered that the students, and even Rembrandt himself, had used only black chalk. And truly, the woman's clothes seemed gaudy, even for Amsterdam.

"It's nothing, Domingo," she said aloud, dismissing her own uneasiness. She tugged at her dress and the rat scampered out, dropping onto the dirt floor and making a quick investigation of everything in the shed. She followed him closely.

"Are you taking me on a tour of your new home?" She laughed. "It's elegant, compared to your last resi-

dence. This glass window is so sunny and there's much
more space!" Domingo ran in and out of a clay flowerpot that lay on its side and then batted at a tangled
piece of string that dangled from a rusty nail.

The curious rat was just about to climb into a large
oval basket filled with straw when a shadow fell across
the doorway. Maria turned to see a young man dressed
in a long brown vest and matching breeches. His loose
white shirt was open at the neck, and he had rolled his
sleeves up to his elbows. Two small books bound in a
leather belt dangled from his hand. His eyes were large
and serious under a wavy fringe of brown hair that
framed his face and fell nearly to his neck. He spoke to
her questioningly in a quiet but steady voice.

"You must be Titus," she ventured in Portuguese,
remembering what Rabbi Menasseh and his wife had
told her of Rembrandt's son.

"And you are Maria," he said. "I thought I'd meet
you yesterday, but you slept like a rock, all through
dinner and past the time when I had to leave for
school. I'm afraid Rabbi Menasseh must have exaggerated my command of his language. I really don't speak
Portuguese too well."

"Far better than my Dutch," she argued.

"But what are you doing in the shed?" Titus asked.
"It's not much of a view."

She was about to answer when Domingo scampered
out from behind a curved shovel and darted into his
apple basket. Titus stepped back in alarm. "A rat! I'll
tell Freeda to put out some—"

"No, no!" she interrupted. "This is Domingo. He
came with me on the ship. He's quite tame. Rem-

brandt put him here so he would be safe. I came out to bring him some food. Please don't tell Freeda."

"How did you ever tame a rat?" Titus asked. Maria scooped Domingo from his basket and held him up. Like his father earlier in the day, the young man was not afraid of the animal but was rather amused and curious.

"Can we take him into the yard?" he asked. "It can't be good for him to be shut in here all day, can it? I'll help you watch him. He won't run away, will he?"

Titus was good at asking questions but rarely waited for an answer. His eyes alive with anticipation, he dropped his books in the shed and darted out the doorway. She followed him willingly. Here was someone she could talk to and a companion who could share Domingo's playfulness. She set the rat on the grass.

Domingo squealed and hopped onto her shoe. She took a piece of cheese from her apron pocket and tossed it on the ground, just a few feet in front of him. He sniffed the cheese hungrily, stretching his body forward, but he couldn't reach the prize without walking. She placed him back on the grass and stepped away. Domingo lifted his feet alternately but wouldn't budge.

"Do you think he doesn't like the feel of the grass?" Titus asked. "Maybe it pinches."

"He was born on the ship, and then I put him in the shed. He never has felt grass before." She came closer to Domingo and picked up the cheese with one hand and the rat with the other. "I've been so mean," she apologized. "Come and ride on my shoulder." She held out her arm and let Domingo find a comfortable perch before giving him the cheese. "I guess we don't have to worry about him running away."

The boy let out a short laugh, so much like his father's, as if he was not accustomed to allowing himself more. He gestured around the limited grassy space. "There's not much here. Just Hendrickje's flower garden."

There was a small area of dirt toward the back of the yard, near a low fence separating the master's property from the house behind it. "Are you growing a vegetable garden?" She followed Titus toward the plot. Someone had raked the earth smooth and it was ready for planting.

"Not this year," he replied. "Usually, Hendrickje grows a few things, but this spring she wasn't up to it."

Maria felt the color rising in her cheeks. "I know," she said. "That's one of the reasons your father wants me to stay and help out, although I haven't been of much use yet. Really, I should go back inside."

She thought of the hateful hours she had spent working in the fields at the monastery. Yet she loved watching the plants grow and blossom, seeing their fruits ripen. It wasn't the work she had disliked, she realized. It was being forced to work so many hours only to serve the results to the ungrateful friars. Having her own garden would be different and would give her a useful way of contributing to the household. It would also get her away from Freeda.

"I could work the garden if someone can get me seeds," she offered. "But I've heard it gets cold here in the winter. It's not too late, is it?"

"I don't think so," Titus said. "But how do you know about gardening? Anyway, we can go to the market tomorrow. I'll bet we can find small plants that have already sprouted, and we'll have a crop before the season ends. What should we plant?"

Again, Titus's questions went unanswered. He disappeared into the shed and returned with a scrap of paper and a piece of chalk. He sat down on the grass next to the fallow garden and propped the paper against his knee.

"This will be your first lesson in Dutch." Maria knelt down next to him and watched as he wrote. "First we'll put in some beans," he said, and wrote *bonen*. He said it out loud and Maria repeated the word.

"Now I know what was stamped on the sacks in the storage room on the ship," she realized. "They said *bonen*. Beans!" She hoped that other Dutch words would be as easy to learn as that.

Titus nodded in approval. "And carrots," he said. "Father loves carrots." He wrote *wortel*. Maria tried the word three times. It started with a *w* but was pronounced as if it began with a *v*. She was only on her second Dutch word and already it was getting difficult. Titus kept planning and writing, and she continued to pucker out the words as best she could. The list included beets, turnips, squash, and cabbage. She hoped there would be enough room for all those vegetables in the garden, and enough room in her brain for all the new words.

But Titus wasn't finished. Now that he had begun, he took the chalk and walked to the fence. In clear letters he wrote *omheining*. Maria tried out the strange sound. "Om-hay-ning," she said, realizing that the word wasn't difficult at all. He moved through the yard, writing on the outhouse, the well, the shed, and inside on the flowerpots and tools. Maria and Titus practiced, laughing whenever she said a word correctly, and laughing harder when she said it wrong. She set Domingo back into his apple basket and left a few pieces of cheese and bread for him. Titus took the saucer and returned with fresh water.

"I really must go in," she said, noticing that the sun was lower in the sky. "I never meant to stay out so long. Freeda might be angry with me. Although I suspect she doesn't like having to share her kitchen with a stranger." She closed the shed door behind her, giving one last look at Domingo as he curled up contentedly in his basket for a nap.

"Freeda is not in charge of the household," Titus declared. "Father says she is lazy as chalk in a box, but Hendrickje never scolds her."

Maria sensed his admiration of his mother, but she was curious as to why he spoke of her by her first name. He referred to Rembrandt as "Father." Could it be an unusual Dutch custom?

When they entered the house, Freeda was standing at a high table facing a heap of potatoes. She pared each one with a small knife, sending the peels flying into the air with exaggerated force. She frowned but said nothing. Maria didn't need words to feel scolded. She could see that Freeda had cleaned the lunch dishes and was now preparing supper. She washed her hands in a tin basin and began to scrape the skins from a pile of carrots waiting on the worktable. Maria had prepared mountains of potatoes and carrots at the monastery. There were so many to feed. But where were the people who would fill the long table in the master's kitchen and eat all the food that would be cooked?

Maria heard voices in the front hallway and thought

she recognized Hendrickje's soft voice speaking with a man. The house had so many visitors. First the rabbi and his wife, then Freeda's secretive friend, and the Lady in Red sneaking up the studio staircase. She was sure there would be nothing suspicious about the last two visitors once she knew the household better.

The speaker in the hallway grew louder. At first Maria thought the rabbi had returned, but this voice was deeper and more demanding.

Titus looked alarmed. "Heer Thyss!" he said, muttering under his breath. He rushed out into the hallway.

Freeda looked smug, raising her eyebrow to indicate she knew something about what was going on. Maria thought she would try to get some information from her. "Thyss?" she asked, questioningly.

"Hmph!" Freeda mocked. She put down the potato she held and rubbed her stubby thumb against her chunky fingers. "*Geld,*" Freeda muttered.

"Money?" Maria asked in Portuguese. Freeda took her apron pocket and turned it inside out. It was empty. She looked at Maria and laughed. Then she plunked the potato she was peeling on top of the pile, stuck the knife into it, and walked out.

The heavy front door closed, and in a moment, Titus guided Hendrickje into the kitchen and eased her into a chair. He poured some water from a blue pitcher and brought it to her. Hendrickje looked pale, and her hands shook as she brought the cup to her lips. The young man spoke to her calmly, and she nodded in agreement.

"Where's Freeda?" Titus asked, but no sooner had he finished his question than the girl appeared in the doorway. She sidled up to the vegetables and began slicing them into a heavy black stock pot.

Titus spoke to Maria. "Hendrickje would like you to go upstairs to the studio and tell Rembrandt and the apprentices to get ready for dinner. It takes them a while to clean up, and they could use your help. Freeda can finish here. Do you know how to reach the attic studio?"

"Shall I go up the outside stairs?"

Titus seemed surprised that she knew about the back stairs. "No," he said tersely. "Go through the foyer. You might have to knock at the studio door a few times. Father hates to be disturbed and often won't open the door unless you persist. Don't let him scare you away or the students will never get their dinner!" He smiled, but the humor in his voice was forced. He, also, had been visibly upset by the visit from Heer Thyss. Could someone as famous as the master have no money to pay his debts? That seemed to be what Freeda would have gossiped if Maria could understand her.

The church clock chimed five times and she was amazed that the afternoon had gone by so quickly. She shouldn't have left the kitchen for so long, and hoped Hendrickje wasn't upset with her. But the visit from Heer Thyss seemed to have taken all her concentration.

"Simply say *avondeten* when my father opens the door. *Avondeten* means 'dinner.' "

Maria walked into the foyer, past the imposing paintings, up the carved staircase and the attic steps, saying *avondeten* over and over to herself. But when she knocked on the closed studio door, Rembrandt shouted, *"Weggaan!"* She remembered the pancake seller who had yelled at her yesterday in the market-place and nearly forgot the new word. She collected herself and knocked again, harder this time, and Rembrandt threw open the door. At first he glared at her angrily but then looked surprised to see who it was. She thought perhaps the master had already forgotten about her.

"*Avondeten,*" she said clearly.

Rembrandt broke into a smile. He held the open door wider and motioned for her to come in. She stood at the back of the class this time and had a perfect view of the drawings propped on every easel. Her eye was drawn to one rough sketch on which she could barely make out the subject. She glanced at a second student's work, this one done with remarkable skill. The drawing was of a half-naked woman pouring water from a pitcher onto her bare feet.

Rembrandt clapped his hands and announced something to the class. They put down their chalk and began to talk and move about. Then Maria saw that the subject of the sketch was a live model. A woman stretched her arms at the front of the room and plunked a pitcher down heavily on the floor, talking loudly in complaining tones. Rembrandt went to help her up, and Maria was jolted into recognition. As the woman pulled a sheet around her bare torso, she saw that it was the Lady in Red.

"Don't be so horrified," the woman said in Portuguese. "Come and help me with my clothes."

Maria was speechless. She obediently followed the woman behind a folding screen set up in the back of the room. The red dress lay crumpled on a pile of pet-

ticoats. The woman pulled a stiff corset up around her
chest and commanded, "Lace!"

Without knowing what to do, Maria began pulling
the laces around tiny hooks. "Tighter!" the lady ordered. "I won't break." Maria pulled the laces tighter
and tied them in a bow when she had finished. The
woman audibly let out her breath. She began pulling
on starched petticoats that tied with a string around
her waist. Maria had never seen such underclothes.

"How do you think artists draw their subjects without real models?" the woman challenged her. "Without people like me, willing to sit for hours on end,
these students would never learn what a human body
looks like. It's life!" she said defiantly. "Real life!" She
pulled on her rustling red dress, pushing her arms into
the tight sleeves. Maria couldn't help but notice that
the woman's skin was pale and flabby under her laced
corset. But the students had drawn her without a flaw,
smooth skin running in sleek lines up her back and
down her arms. She didn't think artists drew real life.
They drew life as they wanted to see it. She thought of
the paintings hanging in the foyer. Peaceful scenes of
golden countrysides and faces of calm, beautiful
women. She had seen life, and that was not it. There
were folds of flab in real life.

"Button!" commanded the woman.

The dress had tiny, round fabric buttons that had to
be forced into narrow loops. The task was tedious, and
Maria wondered who had helped the woman into the
dress in the first place. Surely she hadn't done it alone.
"I didn't know you spoke Portuguese," Maria said timidly when she found her voice.

"How would you know?" the woman mocked her.

"You never spoke to me before." Maria smiled to herself. Domingo did all the talking for us, she remembered. "Actually, I speak Dutch, of course, and Portuguese, Spanish, French, English, and a bit of German. This is Amsterdam, young lady, and one must converse in the tongues of many countries to be successful."

Maria wondered if the Lady in Red was truly successful in what she did. What did she do? Model for artists? Even Maria had done that successfully, and she had scarcely been here two days.

When the last button was fastened, the woman stepped from behind the screen and picked up her shoes. They were red brocade slippers, open at the back, and had a raised wooden heel. That must be what made them click along the cobblestones. She walked toward the door at the back of the studio. The clatter of students folding easels and packing away palettes made the room noisy, and the woman raised her voice so Maria could hear her above the din.

"Rembrandt tells me you're looking for your family."

"Yes," Maria said eagerly. She would tell everyone she could about her parents until she found someone who knew them. "My father's name is Abraham Ben Lazar. I believe he came here from Lisbon six years ago."

"Never heard of him," the woman said, dismissing the name with a disdainful wave of her hand. "And believe me, Dame Margot Prinsenhof knows everybody. But don't worry. If he's in Amsterdam, I'll find out."

Rembrandt approached the woman and said a few words. He opened the door for her and discreetly placed a coin in her hand. Dame Prinsenhof took it and dropped it down the front of her dress.

"In the meantime," she advised, "check all the appropriate places. First, the jail." Maria's stomach turned cold as she remembered her approach to the barred windows near the marketplace. She prayed her parents would not be there. "And, as for your sister, be sure to check the orphanage." Maria would ask Titus about that tomorrow when they went to market. "And don't overlook Ouderkerk," she said finally. She started down the stairs, her hat flopping as she walked and her shoes tucked under her arm.

"What's Ouderkerk, madam?" Maria called after her.

The woman never turned. "Why, it's the Jewish cemetery," she said as Rembrandt closed the door.

11

Choose Life

es!" shouted the deep, booming voice of the crier as he walked along the street announcing the time. "*Zes uur!*" Six o'clock. His call echoed off the brick houses and grew fainter as it reached Maria's ears. Now the church bell echoed the hour with six reverberating peals of its huge bell. Another morning in Rembrandt's house. Another morning without her family.

A full week had passed, and still there was no word. Maria pulled the blanket up to her chin and blinked back tears. As long as she was occupied with the constant activity in the household, she had little time to feel sorry for herself. But in the hours when she was alone in the lavender-scented bed, she could not stop her thoughts from dwelling on her family.

Titus had helped Maria follow Dame Prinsenhof's advice, checking the places where her parents or her sister might have been detained. She remembered the sadness that had engulfed her when she and Titus visited the orphanage that housed the homeless children of the city. They had entered at the heavy wooden gates to inquire if a young Portuguese girl had been given shelter there. A kindly woman had searched her register carefully, but no one by the name of Isobel had been listed and she could recall no children who would fit the description they gave.

Maria had caught a brief glimpse of girls and boys lined up in two orderly rows in the inner courtyard. The children were unnaturally silent, and their heads were down. The girls were all dressed in simple gray dresses with white collars and aprons, and their heads were covered with linen caps. The boys stood as still as statues. Their drab, reddish brown breeches and short, ill-fitting jackets were neatly pressed, and their black caps were set straight upon their heads. It did not seem a joyful place, but Isobel would have been safe there. Maria had felt a heavy weight of disappointment as they left.

Then there was the frightful trip to the jail. Maria had clung to Titus's hand while an unsmiling official with a drooping mustache had scanned several pages in a black log book before announcing that no one from Maria's family had been imprisoned.

Finally, Titus had brought her on the long boat ride to Ouderkerk, where the Jews of the city had been given land for a cemetery. Thankfully, the keeper re-assured her that her parents were not resting among the narrow gravesites marked with stones bearing silent names and blessings etched in Hebrew characters. Now she pushed back the covers and stepped onto the cool tiled floor to dissolve the chilling memory.

Maria draped a shawl over her nightgown, stepped into a pair of wooden clogs, and walked out to the privy. The sun had not yet burned through the damp mist that hung over the yard, and she pulled the shawl

tighter against her shoulders. She stopped first at the
shed and filled Domingo's saucer with fresh water from
the bucket at the well. A few crusts of bread, some
lettuce, and a stick of raw carrot would keep him fed
for the day. She held him close for a moment, nuzzling
his soft, squirming body before leaving. She closed the
door of the shed tightly, knowing that his fear of the
grass would keep him from straying even if she left it
unlatched. Still, she wasn't going to take any chances.

Freeda was clattering dishes onto the long wooden
table when she returned, but it was Saturday, and Hendrickje had told Maria she would not have to work on
the Jewish Sabbath.

I don't have to please Freeda, she reminded herself.
Besides, I'll work tomorrow when she is free to go to
church.

Freeda glared at her as she walked through. The girl
appeared angry at everything Maria did. If she prepared
food, it wasn't done to Freeda's liking. If she washed
dishes, Freeda complained that she hadn't cleaned
them thoroughly. When Maria posed for the master,
Freeda taunted her for being lazy.

But most of all, Freeda resented having her around
the house to walk in on her when she least expected
it. More than once, Maria had found the girl stuffing
her mouth with pilfered food. She had found napkins
filled with wedges of cheese and chunks of bread hidden in out-of-the-way corners. And twice this week
Maria found her standing in the shadows of the shed,
whispering with the narrow-eyed young man she called
her cousin. Freeda's cousin seemed to appear from nowhere, slinking away immediately if Maria chanced
upon them. He never said a word to her, but pulled his

hat down over his face, tugged his jacket closed, and
disappeared. The encounters made Maria uneasy, but
Freeda seemed almost frightened.

She slipped into the blue gabardine dress that Matilda Ben Israel had sent her. It belonged to her son's
wife but hadn't fit since their new baby daughter was
born. It was elegant but not showy, and she loved it for
that very reason. An embroidered linen collar spread
out from its high neckline and covered both the front
and back of the dress. I hope I'll never wear anything
loose and brown again, she thought.

Maria stepped in front of the framed mirror in the
hallway and brushed her hair until it fell in soft waves
over the collar. She wanted to look her best this morning because Matilda and Rembrandt were taking her to
the Portuguese synagogue to hear the service. She had
never seen a formal Sabbath service and remembered a
few prayers only dimly.

She studied her reflection in the mirror. Have I
changed too much for my parents to recognize me? She
looked thoughtfully into her own eyes. Do I look like
my mother now? But she didn't see her mother's face
in her own. Instead she saw Isobel's. We have the same
high cheekbones, she realized, and the same cast to
our eyes. Even my hair falls just as hers does. I haven't
seen my own reflection since I went to the monastery,
but I have looked upon Isobel's face every day. We are
each other's image.

She began to turn away from the mirror, not wanting to confront her sister's likeness, and caught a
glimpse of Freeda's chubby reflection in the corner of
the glass. She had been spying on Maria from the door-

way, not realizing that her face was caught in the mirror, too.

Maria whirled about, crying, *"Weggaan!"* and the girl jumped behind the doorway as if dodging a lightning bolt. How easily Freeda could be scared off. I'm beginning to understand the conversations around me and already I can respond in Dutch to her orders. I'm sure Freeda never expected that.

She waited until she heard the apprentices in the kitchen before she went in for breakfast. Five of them lived in the narrow cubicles in the attic studio and came to all the meals. At noontime, after Rembrandt was pried from the studio, the day apprentices also crowded around the long kitchen table with the family. Eleven students, plus the master, Hendrickje, and Titus made a large, noisy group. After serving the food, Maria and Freeda joined them and they all ate together. Only when there were guests for luncheon or dinner did the apprentices eat without the family. Most of the time Titus joined them, and she liked those meals the best.

This morning Titus's voice, still high pitched and childlike, rose above the others. They trailed off into silence when Maria entered, and she hesitated before their stares.

"It's not rude for artists to stare," Titus joked. "It's just that Father usually chooses such homely models that the students must look long and hard at you to be able to remember your lovely face when they are forced to draw the next one."

He summarized his teasing in Dutch for the students, and there were loud guffaws at the truth of his remarks. "When you arrived," one of them said to her, speaking slowly, "we wondered what had possessed the master that he brought us a model we would enjoy looking at. The others are fat and wrinkled!" He gestured with his hands to be sure she understood.

"What's this talk of ugly models?" bellowed Rembrandt as he strode into the room. He pulled a chair out roughly, scraping its legs against the floor, and sat down heavily. "Life cannot be made beautiful just for your eyes. You must paint the toad with all its warts." The students exchanged furtive looks, as if they had heard this before. He piled his plate with bread, cheese, and cold meats, and Freeda hurried to pour him a mug of tea. She walked around the table, pouring tea for each of the young men, but stopped when she got to Maria. She thumped the teapot down and walked off. Without a word, Maria poured her own tea.

"Where is Hendrickje this morning?" Titus asked, and she heard the concern in his voice.

"I tried not to wake her. There's no reason for her to be up this early. She needs more rest than she is getting. You boys may take a holiday this morning while I'm at the Portuguese synagogue. And I mean a holiday out of the house. I want Hendrickje to sleep." The apprentices chattered happily in anticipation of the free day, while Rembrandt turned his gaze on Maria. "Are you ready, child? Matilda should be here shortly."

Maria finished her bread and sipped at the tea. Her stomach was jumpy at the prospect of attending the Sabbath services. Rabbi Menasseh had explained that this was the morning of his monthly sermon, and he would be sure to ask the congregation about her parents while they were all assembled. "Surely we will find a relative or an old neighbor who knows your family," he said confidently. Maria hung on his hopes.

There was a soft rapping at the kitchen door and Rembrandt got up from the table, wiping his hands on his pants. A small, greasy spot appeared just where his fingers rubbed across his thigh, and Maria noticed that his hair was unkempt and sticking out rather wildly from his floppy beret. He needed Hendrickje to smooth his appearance. Already she had observed how little the master thought of his own image. Often he would try to rush off on business wearing his studio smock covered with a kaleidoscope of paint stains. Hendrickje had a way of gently chiding him and helping him out of the messy smock and into a neatly brushed coat. Once she had seen Hendrickje sit him down on the bench in the foyer and brush his unruly hair, clucking at him lovingly.

"Come, come," prodded Matilda Ben Israel, clapping her hands together. "We shall be late and Menasseh will . . ." Maria didn't understand the last word, but she understood the tone.

Out the door and up the street they hurried, with the rabbi's wife speaking a combination of Dutch and Portuguese so both Maria and Rembrandt could understand her. Her hands gestured like fluttering birds as she talked, and Maria doubted that the tiny woman could speak if her hands were tied behind her.

"We've been in this synagogue for fifteen years already," she explained. "We have a school for the children and a few temporary housing units for the new families that keep arriving." She turned to Rembrandt as they crossed the bridge and laid her fingers on his sleeve. "This synagogue was finished in 1639, the same year you and Saskia moved into the new house."

Rembrandt's eyes seemed to look far across the canal. "Saskia," he murmured. Maria guessed that must be his first wife. Freeda had told her Titus's mother had died, and yet Hendrickje was such a loving mother. It was hard to imagine he had ever known any other.

Knots of people converged on the street, all heading in the same direction. Maria heard animated conversations in the smooth Portuguese words she was used to, so different from the hard, guttural sounds of Dutch. She began to scan the faces of the people around her. One of them might be a playmate from her childhood in Lisbon, or a neighbor, a cousin. Her heart raced. Any one of them might be her mother or father.

Rembrandt was scrutinizing the faces as well, but he was viewing them with an artist's eye. "Ah," he breathed, pointing openly to a slender, bearded young man who approached from a side street, "the true face of Jesus. Look at his eyes."

"Shh," Matilda scolded him. "He's always looking for new faces, new models. I think we can find our entire congregation in Rembrandt's paintings." Maria thought of a painting that rested against the wall in the studio. It depicted Jesus and his disciples. She now understood what had drawn her to the painting and held her. Every one of the men in the painting looked somehow familiar. Were those the faces of neighbors she had known in Lisbon?

The trio crossed a steep brick bridge. Rembrandt pulled himself along by grasping at the black iron railing that spanned it and leaning heavily on his walking

stick. He wheezed slightly with the exertion. Maria
wondered how old he was. Matilda Ben Israel seemed
no older, but her trim form marched steadily along as
if the bridge were flat.

A cobblestone square stretched before them and was
filled with the bustle of people in a hurry. Unlike the
floppy beret Rembrandt favored, the men wore wide-
brimmed hats that curved jauntily at the sides. They
escorted finely dressed women whose heads were covered by feathered hats or loose silken hoods. Most of
the men had neatly trimmed beards that covered their
chins and connected to slender mustaches. Their
cheeks were shaved clean. "My father had a beard like
that," she said. She scrutinized the face of each man
that passed.

"The Sephardic face," Rembrandt declared. "It
seems every Jewish man from Spain or Portugal arrives
with just such a beard. It's like a uniform. We'll never
find your father by looking for his beard."

"Rembrandt exaggerates, child," Matilda said. "But
we certainly don't resemble these pale Dutchmen who
spend most of the year in front of a warm fire!" She
slowed her steps as they approached an imposing brick
building that loomed taller than the trees in the
square. "Here we are."

A sleek carriage, pulled by four matched horses,
clattered up to the door of the building and stopped.
The driver stepped down and opened the carriage door,
assisting a frail woman dressed in rustling blue silk. Her
face was creased with wrinkles, like a washed apron
waiting to be ironed smooth, and her white hair was
pulled back in a tight bun. She made her way up the
steps, stopping at the top to rest on one of the benches

that framed the doorway. The carriage rolled smoothly away, making a soft creaking sound barely heard above the clopping of the horses' hooves.

"Now, that's one luxury I have never been able to afford," the master grumbled. "Imagine having your own carriage to carry you about the city. I'm sure Hendrickje would get out more if she could ride in privacy."

"Walking in the fresh air is good for us," said the rabbi's wife as she led them up the steps. She smiled at the elderly woman who called out in Hebrew as the congregants entered at the door. *"Shabbat Shalom!"* she sang out cheerily.

"Now, there is a greeting you wouldn't hear shouted in the streets in many cities," Rembrandt remarked, forgetting about the carriage. "For all its faults, at least I can say my Calvinist church is tolerant of those who hold other beliefs." His tone became cynical. "It's amazing, really, for a faith that won't tolerate any dissension from its own members."

They entered the darkened sanctuary and Maria drew in her breath. It was magnificent. Polished wooden beams stretched under huge domed arches in the ceiling. Her eyes traveled up, up, past the hanging brass candelabra filled with slender white tapers, along the open balcony that ran along both sides, up to the tall windows that allowed filtered light to float down onto the burnished wooden ark and the raised prayer table before it.

Matilda beamed proudly, reading her face. "It is beautiful, isn't it? For the first time, we can worship in a temple that stands before both God and the people. There is no more hiding in dark cellars or stifling secret rooms. In Amsterdam, Jews are truly free. We say this is the New Jerusalem, for if we cannot be in the Holy Land, this is as close as we could hope to be."

"My father took me to a few secret prayer meetings," Maria said. "They were always late at night, and I was too young and too tired to really understand, but I learned a little about the holidays, and my mother taught me the blessings for the Friday night candles." Now she was among her own people and was free to learn all that she had been denied.

She tried to tell Rembrandt in her halting Dutch what it had been like before she escaped. "At the monastery, we older children tried to remember holidays, prayers, rituals and tell the younger ones." She smiled at a trick she had nearly forgotten. "Every December we guessed when it might be time to celebrate Hanukkah. Then we mumbled 'Mea Hanukkah,' for a whole week all through the Latin 'Mea culpa' prayers. The friars never noticed." Rembrandt laughed, and Matilda looked surprised. "It seemed a wonderful gift we had given each other, simply to fool the friars and remember a celebration we had all loved."

Rembrandt looked toward the wooden benches that radiated alongside the prayer table. "Ah, there's Bonus," he said. "I'll sit with him." He left Maria and Matilda to make their way to the balcony where the women sat together, conversing quietly behind their waving lace fans.

Maria's foot scratched across sand covering the wide wooden floor planks. "It's not that we're too lazy to sweep," Matilda said with a smile. "This is sand brought from Jerusalem to remind us of our roots, our Promised Land. Members of our congregation who are merchants arrange to bring bags of it from their travels there. We scatter it sparingly, but we always use it."

A respectful hush swept across the temple as Rabbi Menasseh Ben Israel stepped up to the prayer table and began the service. Maria leaned forward on the polished bench, straining to hear every word he spoke, but the sounds of Hebrew were almost as unrecognizable as the Dutch she was struggling to learn. Before each prayer was spoken, the rabbi explained its meaning and purpose. Gradually she settled back and closed her eyes until only the rabbi's voice filled her senses.

There was a scraping of shoes and the swishing of polished fabric as the congregation members rose to their feet. Rabbi Menasseh and two other men bowed and prayed before the carved ark that held the scroll of the Torah, the sacred words by which they lived. The doors were opened and an exquisitely embroidered curtain was parted slowly. The rabbi cradled the Torah against his arm and people began singing joyfully as he paraded it around the room. Men reached forward, touching the precious scroll reverently with the tassels that fringed their prayer shawls.

Maria didn't know the song, but a sense of celebration rushed through her. She had felt that emotion only once before when she had looked out at the harbor of Recife and felt the closeness of freedom for herself and her sister. If only she had kept Isobel close to her, they would be sharing this moment together.

The rabbi returned to the prayer table. The silver crowns that decorated the wooden dowels of the scroll were removed and its velvet cover was laid aside. He unfurled the scroll until the cryptic Hebrew calligraphy could be seen. He held it aloft, as if in triumph. "This is the Torah that Moses placed before the people of Israel to fulfill the word of God."

The scroll was lowered onto the prayer table and the rabbi called upon one after another of several men in the congregation. Each recited a prayer and then read aloud from the holy book, keeping the place with a thin silver pointer and chanting in repetitive tones.

When the reading ended and the Torah was replaced in the ark, Rabbi Menasseh faced the congregation. He quoted a passage from Deuteronomy and explained its meaning. His voice rose from deep within him and resonated across the cavernous space. The women stopped fanning themselves, and not even a child's foot scratched across the floor.

"Moses reminds the Jews that God has worked many wonders to bring them out of the land of Egypt and that they must now enter a covenant with God. Moses might well speak these same words to you. The Lord has brought you out of the bondage of your lives in Spain and Portugal to the freedom and safety of Amsterdam. Now each of you must renew your covenant with the Lord in your own heart." There was a murmur of approval.

Rabbi Menasseh looked up into the balcony as he spoke. His eyes settled lovingly upon his wife for a brief moment and then scanned the gallery, enfolding each person in his gaze. "Moses explains that the most important choice each person must make is to follow good ways and be rewarded with a full life in a prosperous land. In Moses' words, 'I call heaven and earth to witness that I have set before you life and death, the blessing and the curse; therefore choose life.' "

Maria felt the emotion of Rabbi Menasseh's words. I

tried to choose life, she thought, to choose the freedom to follow my faith, but I have lost my family. I can
control my faith but not my destiny.

The rabbi's voice softened. "I ask you to choose life
but I also tell you that you must shape your own future.
We cannot expect God to answer our every prayer." It
seemed as if he heard her thoughts.

Maria leaned forward, feeling the warm air that
wafted in at the open doors of the entryway below.
"Many times you have opened your homes to one of
our people who also seeks freedom here. Other times
you have generously donated your hard-earned guilders
to support a destitute family or ransom our countrymen
from the hands of the Inquisition. Today, I have a sim-
pler request for your help." Maria felt Matilda's warm
hand cover hers. "We have among us a new congre-
gant, one who has truly chosen life. Maria Ben Lazar
was taken from her family in Lisbon after the Decree
of 1648, and she and her sister were sent to a monastery in Brazil." There was a buzz of conversation and
the women looked sympathetically at Maria.

The rabbi continued. "You have heard these stories.
Some of you have lived them. Maria has made a har-
rowing escape and is now safe among us, but she needs
your efforts to make her life whole again. If any of you
have word of her young sister, Isobel, we need your
information. Some of you must have known the girls'
parents, Eva and Abraham Ben Lazar. Abraham was
adviser to the king of Portugal, and we have reason to
believe he and his wife sought refuge here in Amsterdam. If you can help us in this search, you may find
Maria living with our good friend Rembrandt van Rijn,
or you may speak to me." There were smiles and nods

as the congregants spotted the master sitting among
them. He was apparently a familiar guest.

Maria prayed someone might suddenly stand and an-
nounce that he knew her parents. But there was only
silence. She barely heard the chorus of voices that
joined in the concluding prayers and rose unsteadily
after Rabbi Menasseh wished his congregants a day
filled with the peace of the Sabbath.

"Don't lose hope," Matilda said when they were
once again standing in the courtyard. "Just because no
one came forward immediately doesn't mean Menasseh's request will go unanswered. Someone may wish
to give their information privately."

Maria couldn't help feeling discouraged. "Why
would anyone need to hide what they know?"

"There are many here with much they wish to forget," she explained. "Look," she smiled, pointing into
the crowd, "do you see Rembrandt talking to that
young man?" Maria turned and saw the master talking
earnestly with the youth he had observed when they
entered the courtyard earlier. "I can guarantee he will
be sitting in Rembrandt's studio before the week is out.
And then you will surely see him on canvas as a young
Jesus."

Rembrandt and another man approached, and the
master had a look of distracted satisfaction on his face.
"This is Dr. Ephraim Bonus." Maria nodded politely.
She remembered Rabbi Menasseh said the doctor
would probably know of her parents if they were living
in the city.

"Come," said Dr. Bonus. "I'll walk you back to the
Breestraat. Heer van Rijn has promised me a mug of
cold beer and a chance to see his lovely Hendrickje."

He turned to Maria. "You have survived an arduous journey, young lady. That shows courage."

"I don't feel courageous." She looked down at the uneven gray and red cobblestones as she walked. "I have lost my sister, and if my parents aren't in Amsterdam, where will I find them?"

"You must give it time," he said.

"But I've already given six years. Don't you recognize the name Ben Lazar?" she asked hopefully.

Dr. Bonus shook his head. "I am sorry."

The group crossed the bridge and headed onto the wide avenue that led to Rembrandt's house. "Maybe my parents chose a Dutch name when they came here," Maria suggested. "Titus says some families have. Think, Dr. Bonus. Haven't you met a couple who lost their children to the Inquisition?"

Dr. Bonus hesitated and his silence was broken only by the tapping of Rembrandt's cane. Then he said, "Yes, child, I have. Too many to count."

12

News from the Sea

on't chew the carrot tops," Maria scolded. She moved Domingo closer to the bean plants that she had just staked with twine. A few thin beans hung from each plant, and folded white blossoms promised more to come.

"Stay there," she said, though she knew the rat wouldn't stray from the soft earth of the garden plot. He still hated the pinchy feel of grass and would jump onto her shoes if she put him on the lawn. She was glad for the security his fears gave her. She could keep Domingo with her whenever she worked in the garden, and he stayed within its boundaries as if he were bound by a brick wall.

Maria walked to the compost pile at the end of the yard and added the bunch of weeds she had just pulled. The plants had grown quickly in the few weeks she had tended them, and she was excited by the prospect of fresh vegetables that wouldn't have to be purchased at the market. Nevertheless, she had expected to be gone before the seedlings would bear fruit. She had been sure she'd find Isobel and her parents before then. The bigger the plants grew, the more her hopes shriveled.

Maria wiped perspiration from her face with the corner of her apron. The church bell had just tolled eleven times, and the coolest part of the day was over. The master said Amsterdam had never been this hot so many days in a row. Normally, they wore cloaks in the evening all through the summer, he'd explained, but this year July was oppressive. To Maria, the heat here was nothing like the intense heat of Brazil, yet the people of Amsterdam could not tolerate it. Many were suffering from heat sickness, and there was fear of influenza spreading across the city.

Maria scooped Domingo away from the dangling pea pods and settled him on her shoulder. "Peas," she said, enunciating the Dutch word carefully. "If I have to learn Dutch, so do you, my little friend."

Back at the shed, she gave him fresh water and set him down in front of his apple crate. He stretched one back leg and opened his mouth in a lazy yawn, then crawled in and curled up to sleep. Maria latched the door behind her, washed her hands in the basin by the kitchen door, and entered.

"Take off your shoes, Rat-Girl!" Freeda howled. It hadn't taken long for Freeda to discover that Domingo was housed in the shed, and she expressed her revulsion daily. Maria had tried to explain that Domingo wasn't like any wild rat from the docks, but the housekeeper retorted that Maria was crazy if she believed that.

This morning, Freeda was down on her hands and knees, a scrub brush and bucket of soapy water beside her. Maria might have felt sorry for her, scrubbing on such a sweltering day, but she could see that Freeda hadn't moved from the spot she had been washing when Maria first went outside over an hour ago. She had learned Freeda's tricks. The girl worked hard and looked exhausted whenever Hendrickje or any of the family checked her, but whenever she was alone, she'd leave her tasks to gorge on hoarded bits of food.

Maria removed her clogs and set them outside the door. Then she skirted the soapy spots on the floor and turned toward the back parlor where Hendrickje had left some clothes to be mended.

"Go and rest yourself, Your Majesty," Freeda taunted. "A bit of light sewing will be just the thing. Can I bring you a cool mug of beer?"

Maria had hoped that mastering even a few Dutch phrases would make it easier to get along with Freeda, but it only made it easier for them to argue. If her years at the monastery had taught her anything, it was how to hold her tongue. Nothing would change if she argued better than Freeda. And it infuriated the serving girl when Maria appeared undisturbed by her insults.

Suddenly Freeda fell to scrubbing in big sloshy circles, water spinning out across the floor. Maria looked up to see Hendrickje in the doorway. She moved slowly and deliberately these past weeks, as her body grew heavier with the growing baby. Her face was flushed with the heat, and damp ringlets of hair clung to her forehead.

"I must go out," she said distractedly. She clutched a letter tightly in her hand. The red wax seal had been broken, but Maria thought she could see the fragments of an elaborate cross imprinted on it.

"Shall I call the master?" Maria offered. She knew he wouldn't want Hendrickje walking about the city in the sultry air.

"No," she said quickly, and Maria thought she saw fear widen Hendrickje's eyes. But then she softened her voice and spoke more calmly. "He's printing the etchings he made of you and heaven knows we need the money they will fetch. If we don't settle the debt with Heer Thyss soon, he'll take back the house and we'll have no place to live. Whatever you do, don't interrupt Rembrandt. It's nothing, really."

But whatever message had arrived was surely important enough to call Hendrickje out of the house immediately and had shaken her normally placid demeanor.

"Let me go with you then, Hendrickje. It's too hot for you to be out alone."

"No, Maria. I'll need you to go to market for me this morning. Titus is off with his friends, and I really can't wait for him to return. Do you think you can manage yourself?"

Freeda sat back on her heels. "I can do the marketing," she volunteered.

Hendrickje surveyed the half-washed floor and the puddles of water. "I need you to finish the floor, Freeda, and I see you're not nearly done."

The girl looked gloomily at the scrub brush in her hand, but Hendrickje ignored her. "I know you've never done the marketing alone, Maria, but I think you've done it with Titus or me often enough. It's important, or I wouldn't ask."

Maria silently reviewed the list of Dutch words she had heard them use to purchase the day's provisions. They always offered less than the seller asked at first or waited until their purchases had been placed in their shopping basket before bargaining down to the final price. That would be the hardest task. Hendrickje pulled a list of items from her pocket and gave it to Maria with a handful of coins. "I must leave. Freeda, tell Rembrandt not to worry."

Maria hooked her work apron on a peg near the kitchen doorway. She took the straw market basket from a shelf and looked at Hendrickje's receding back. She walked with an ungainly gait, shifting her weight from one leg to the other as if it were a chore to put one foot down before lifting the other. Maria was certain the mistress shouldn't be out walking in her delicate health, especially in the heat of the day, but it was too late. Whatever had called her away, it was urgent.

Maria latched the bottom half of the double door behind her, leaving the top half open for any slight breeze that might find its way into the kitchen. "Don't hurry, Rat-Girl," Freeda called after her. "Have a nice stroll."

But Maria knew that it was Freeda who would be enjoying a long respite as soon as she had the house to herself again. *I wonder if the floor will be washed by the time I return.*

Then she began to think of the task before her. *I know the way clearly now,* she reassured herself. She was not so afraid of getting lost as she was of the crush of people in the busy marketplace or of being deceived about the price of the food she purchased. She barely knew the money system and would have to count her change carefully.

Maria headed up the Breestraat and across the first canal bridge. She looked at the cool water that stretched out on either side. When she had first arrived

in Amsterdam she had been amazed that so many rivers ran in unbending lines through the city. Now she
nearly laughed at her mistake. When she and Titus
had taken the ferry to Ouderkerk, he had explained
they were canals. They had been dug over many years
to keep the low-lying land dry and provide an easy way
to get about the city in boats. Maria crossed the second
bridge and knew she was getting closer to the square.
As the canals became narrower, the collection of refuse
dumped into them gave off a fierce odor. It would wash
out to sea eventually, but she found it hard to understand how the tidy citizens could keep their streets and
homes so clean and allow the canals to fester.

The rows of narrow houses grew thicker, and people
clogged the streets. Maria simply could not get used to
the congestion of the city, the feeling that everything
was closing in upon her. The rooms at the monastery
were big and cool, and as soon as you stepped outside
there were fields and trees as far as you could see. Still,
I should remember that in the confines of the city, I
am free to go where I wish. The forest around the monastery was really a barrier that kept us prisoners.

She crossed the last canal, worried about the task
ahead. Hendrickje is counting on me.

Hendrickje and Titus usually bought from the same
vendors, and Maria tried to remember the location of
each one. There was less chance that she would be
treated rudely or cheated if she kept to the sellers who
knew she came from the van Rijn household.

She looked over the list carefully: onions, carrots,
small wheel of Edam cheese, four loaves of bread, large
smoked haddock. I'll start with the baker, for although
I need four loaves, they are light. She pushed her way

through the crowd, using her basket as a prod to make a path. She walked toward the shady arcade where breads were displayed in huge straw baskets.

"Four, please," she said, pointing to the basket that held the dark, round loaves that Hendrickje favored. The seller squinted at Maria, as if trying to see if she looked familiar. Then she took the basket and began stacking bread in it rapidly, the veins on her gnarled hands rippling with every motion. Maria watched carefully.

"Wait," she interrupted, as the third loaf was thrust into the basket. She pointed to the bread and shook her head. "Not that one."

"It's not burnt," the old woman protested. "It's just dark." Maria repeated the word "burnt" in her head, trying to remember it for the next time. But she was firm. She shook her head again, and the woman gave a sigh of resignation and took the loaf out. Before handing her the basket, the woman said, "One guilder."

Hendrickje had occasionally paid a guilder for just three loaves of bread, so she drew the heavy coin from her pocket and paid the old woman without argument. The bread seller grinned. "You're a sharp-eyed one," she said approvingly. Then she dropped the slightly burned loaf on top of the others. "Here, you'll make a pudding for the mistress with this."

Maria felt a sense of success in her shopping skills. Five loaves of bread for one guilder was a good bargain, and truly, she thought, the loaf I rejected wasn't badly burned. Just a bit overdone. She moved to the center of the market, looking for a certain vegetable stand, one hand held protectively over the basket. The mar-

ket was always filled with noisy jostling shoppers, but
today the din seemed excessive.

She pushed her way toward the young vegetable
seller Titus favored. She stood behind a fat woman
whose rump jiggled as she leaned forward, squeezing
the peppers and onions critically. The seller was politely trying to keep the woman from disturbing her
display or damaging the produce. "Please, madam,"
she admonished, "I can get whatever you like." But the
fat woman dropped a green pepper carelessly on top of
the onions and grabbed at another one.

Behind the filled wheelbarrows the young seller had
placed her baby daughter into a wooden crate. The
little girl looked out at the busy market with blue eyes
as big as the painted blue bowls in the master's
kitchen. She fixed her curious stare on Maria and let
out a gurgle. The fat woman dropped an onion onto
the neat pile of potatoes and waddled off with a dis-
gusted frown.

"It's bedlam here today," the seller commented. Maria smiled uncertainly. She didn't understand what the
young woman had said. "A ship's come in, and there's
been so much commotion. It seems the whole city's
come to see her. Such a fuss."

Now Maria realized why the marketplace seemed
noisier and more crowded than usual. Ships came in
regularly, but some drew more attention than others.
She wondered where this one had come from. Titus
had told her how many of them traveled around the
world buying spices and exotic fruits, but she knew he
was only fascinated by these stories because he had
never been confined on a tossing, rolling ship before.
Maria would never wish for the life of a sailor.

She told the seller what she needed and watched her pick out the vegetables carefully. There was a bit of bargaining, and finally Maria felt she was given a good price. She thanked the woman and pushed back into the crowd.

As she headed closer to the pier to buy the fish and cheese, she saw Dame Prinsenhof fluttering over a colorful variety of cut flowers. In spite of the heat, she was dressed in rustling yellow taffeta from head to foot. Maria realized that all the woman's clothes were basically the same. Only their colors changed. Maria skirted around the marketplace, not wanting to spend any time trading empty pleasantries with the overbearing woman. She had just added the cheese to her purchases when Dame Prinsenhof saw her.

"Hello!" the woman called shrilly, waving an enormous bouquet of bright yellow sunflowers. She swooped up as Maria began haggling with the fish peddler over a pungent smoked haddock displayed on a bed of straw. Glassy eyes stared unseeing from the scaly creature. Maria dreaded having to carry it all the way home, but Hendrickje fancied serving the fish cold. It was the third time that week she had planned it for dinner.

Dame Prinsenhof draped her free arm around Maria's shoulder as she concluded her bargain and waited for the fish to be wrapped in layers of paper. "My dear," she said with a tone of confidentiality, "I have news."

There was a long pause while the woman smiled with self-importance. Maria trembled to think of all the possible pieces of news she wanted to hear. The woman lowered her voice and whispered loudly, "*The Valck* has come in."

"*The Valck?*" Maria repeated, draping the limp package of fish across the top of her basket. Then the impact of the news hit her. She gripped the heavy basket tightly, as if holding it would steady her. "That's the lost ship! It might be Isobel's ship!"

"As if I didn't know," the woman declared. "Can't you see what an uproar the city is in?" Maria turned toward the dock. The excited group that milled around was different from the crowd of workers that usually converged on a returning ship. There were gentlemen waving sheafs of papers, families calling, children crying, businessmen arguing, and two burly sheriffs trying to control the raucous group.

Maria rushed toward the anchored ship, fighting against the crowd. Everyone was shouting questions, but she couldn't hear any of the answers. She was held to the fringe of the group and was nearly giving up hope of getting through when a deep voice shouted, "Isobel!"

Maria whirled around and saw a burly man rushing toward her. Suddenly he looked startled and stopped a few feet away. He looked confused, and then muttered in Portuguese, "Desculpe. Excuse me, I thought you were someone else."

He turned and began to move off, but Maria rushed up behind him. "Wait!" she called. "What do you know of my sister Isobel?"

The man peered at her intently and scratched his thick, curly beard. "You are Isobel's sister?" he asked softly. "I'm Cado, the ship's cook. Izzy, I mean Isobel, worked with me until she . . . until she was taken." A slow, pained smile turned up the edges of his mouth, and Maria saw a few isolated teeth rimming his gums. He pulled a piece of charred cloth from his pocket and opened it to reveal a strand of silky black hair. A cold chill crept up Maria's neck when she realized the blackened cloth was a piece of Isobel's frock and the hair curled inside matched her own.

Cado moved toward the chipped and blackened hull of *The Valck*. "Come with me," he said. "I have much to tell you."

13

Cado's Story

ado pulled out a low stool for Maria and lowered his burly frame onto the floor of the cook room. The double door was open wide and she looked across the vacant deck. *The Valck* was much the same as the ship she had traveled on, but a thick beam had been lashed onto the broken main mast with rope. Charred patches darkened the deck, and splintered bits of wood along the rail testified to its hazardous voyage.

"I just can't think with these things on," Cado complained, pulling off his boots. He rubbed the soles of his feet and wiggled his toes with relief. "I never pretended to have fine manners," he said, by way of excuse.

"What about Isobel?" Maria said impatiently. She didn't care about the man's manners or his feet. She had followed him onto the ship to learn about her sister. The smoky odor of the haddock in her market basket reminded her that she had to hurry back to the master's before the fish spoiled in the heat. "Do you know where she is?"

"There's no clear answer to that," he said, and Maria felt her heart sink. "She was with me for a time, though, and I can tell you what happened."

At least he had seen Isobel, and knew something about her escape. She had to let the man speak without rushing him.

"I never saw her get onto the ship, so I don't know how she managed that, but she was a clever one, and she made it past the sailors at the gangplank. After about three days at sea I heard there was a stowaway, just a slip of a girl the men said. She'd been holed up under the sloop we keep on deck." Cado smiled. "She was small enough to fit quite comfortably, I expect, and she must've known no one would be touching that sloop for weeks."

"Well, then how did they find her?" Maria asked, frowning.

"I'm getting to it," Cado assured her. "It seems one of the youngsters from the passenger deck was sneaking food and water to her. Eventually, a ship hand grew suspicious."

"But I had given her enough to last several days," Maria interrupted. "I didn't let her go without provisions."

"I can't tell you about that, miss," Cado said, shaking his head. "I can tell you for a plain fact, though, that a sailor caught her reaching for a cup of water that had been set out next to the sloop. When they pulled her out, and the captain came aft to decide what to do, the Jewish families spoke up for her. Lucky for her, too, because she was mighty sick, as I hear it."

"Seasick, you mean?" Maria asked.

"Nothing like that." The cook laughed. "Why, I watched her weather a storm that made even the sailors retch. She had a strong stomach, that one. Born to sail, I told her." He chuckled at the memory and then grew serious again. "It was a festering sore on her back, I heard."

Maria remembered the blow her sister had received the morning they escaped. "On our last morning in Recife, one of the friars came into the barn where we were staying and found us still asleep. He kicked Isobel to wake her up. She was cut, and there was no time to clean it. We had to get away as soon as the friars left us alone. I was afraid the ships would sail without us."

Cado seemed to understand. "Of course you had to get away. There's no blame for that, except for the friar who kicked her. But that blow may have saved her in the long run. You see, she was feverish when they found her and she passed out right in front of the captain. That's when the Jews offered to care for her. The captain was relieved to have her off his conscience. He never took kindly to children, anyway. Found them a nuisance. . . ."

"So she was cured," Maria interrupted, trying to keep the cook focused on his story. "But how did you get to know her?"

He scratched under his arm. "I told you she was a smart one. She made a deal with the captain to work to pay her passage. Otherwise he threatened to ship her back to Brazil as soon as we docked. Anyway, she showed up at the door here, ready to peel potatoes."

Maria couldn't hold back a smile. "That's one thing we've both had a lot of practice with."

Beads of perspiration lined Cado's forehead, and he wiped them with his sleeve. "It's too hot for Amsterdam, even if it is July," he complained. "Feels more like Brazil."

"I can't stay much longer," Maria urged him, "and I've got to know where my sister is."

"I've been told more than once I have a wandering mind," he admitted. "Just keep me pointed in the right direction, though, and eventually I'll spill it all out."

"So Isobel worked for you in the kitchen?"

"Got to be good friends, we did," Cado said with pride. "But she was keeping something inside, holding back. I could sense it, but I didn't guess her secret. It came out during the storm, but then it was too late."

Maria remembered the storm and how her ship was tossed upon the crashing waves as if it would break into slivers. She shivered at the memory of how dizzy and sick she had been and how afraid of being drowned in the violent seas. But she hadn't forgotten Isobel. She had prayed for her sister's safety and her own.

"What was it?" she asked.

"She figured out that the first mate and the helmsman had deliberately set us off course. Turns out they'd made a deal with Spanish privateers to sell off the Jewish passengers to the Inquisition." He spat on the floor. "It was no better than making a pact with the devil! Izzy learned of it in bits and pieces and finally put it all together. I could hardly believe her, but just as she was heading below to warn her friends, the fog lifted and there were the cannons of a Spanish caravel aimed straight at us. The first shot they fired nearly blew us to the bottom of the sea."

Cado sighed and dropped his hands between his legs, where they still gestured weakly as he spoke. "She couldn't do anything, then. *The Valck* couldn't even defend itself. The surprise attack had been perfectly executed, and the storm had been a handy disguise."

"Was there a battle?" Maria asked, her eyes wide with fright. Her stomach fluttered with trepidation at what had happened to her sister.

"If you can call it that," he reflected. "Within half an hour, our mast was severed and the captain ordered the crew to raise the white flag of surrender.

"But I hadn't given up on Izzy," he said earnestly. "I was sure I could hide her from the privateers. I got her dressed up as a cabin boy from boots to hat, and burned that ragged frock to cinders. She let me cut her hair, too, though I didn't give her time to protest." He sighed. "That was surely the hardest thing I ever did. All those silky black curls, just like yours. I should have known you couldn't be Isobel when I saw you on the dock. I'm sure her hair hasn't grown back yet."

Maria fingered the singed piece of cloth he had handed her on the dock and the soft lock of Isobel's hair. She thought of her sister's clothes burning in the stove that now sat cold and empty next to her. "Cado, you must try to remember something," she said. "Did you burn Isobel's chemise, too?"

"I had forgotten about that," he said. "It was a funny thing. She seemed almost glad to watch the frock go up in flames, but she wouldn't take off that chemise. Only shoved it into the breeches." He looked directly at Maria again. "I remember she said her sister had made it for her and she wouldn't part with it, no matter what."

Maria felt a rush of love for Isobel. I always scolded her for not thinking ahead, but it seems she thought carefully all through her voyage. So many choices, so many challenges, and Isobel had met them all.

"There were more than sentimental reasons to keep that shift," Maria explained. "You see, I had managed to save a pair of silver hair combs that I had been wearing when we were first taken by the soldiers in Portugal. The night before Isobel and I stowed away, I sewed them into the seams of her chemise." She remembered the darkness that had enveloped them in the barn as they made their plans. "Isobel cried when I told her we would have to travel on separate ships. I told her we'd be together again in just a few weeks, but that if anything happened to me, the combs would help our parents recognize her. Or, if necessary, she could sell them. She wouldn't let you burn the chemise because she was afraid of losing those combs."

Cado reached out and put his rough hand on Maria's shoulder. "I almost saved her," he said, and she could see the pain on his face. "I really tried."

Maria swallowed hard and tried to focus on the cook's story. "Tell me the rest."

"The privateers came aboard and crowded all the passengers and crew onto the deck." He gestured to the open door of the cook room. "Izzy and I stood here. I was sure they'd never pick her out. But the first mate had planned everything. He presented the Spanish captain with a list of the Jewish passengers and told him about the stowaway. Why, every name was spelled out, just as plain as day. Isobel watched the families who had cared for her being herded forward by the privateers. And then the Spanish captain baited her. 'Is the stowaway a Jew or a baptized Christian?' he demanded. Before I could do anything, Izzy stepped forward and announced, 'A Jew.' "

Maria held her breath. All the years that the sisters were at the monastery, she had tried to teach Isobel about their heritage, but she had never been sure that her sister accepted it. Now she saw that at some point, perhaps during her voyage from Brazil, she had found her faith. But Maria didn't know if she felt pride or grief. If not for that decision, Isobel would be with her now. She remembered Rabbi Menasseh's sermon. In the words of Moses, Isobel had chosen life, but had God rewarded her?

Cado looked distressed. "I couldn't get her back after that," he said. "Do you see? She had chosen. There was nothing more I could do."

Now it was Maria's turn to comfort the man who had tried to save her sister. "There was nothing else that either of us could have done."

"She stepped into that group of scared families and they welcomed her with love. I could see it. And they walked proudly together, even as they climbed over the side to the rowboats that would take them away. None of them knew what might happen, but they seemed to have an inner faith that somehow they would be saved. Isobel must have believed that, too. I watched her from the railing as they disappeared toward the caravel. She sat up straight in the sloop next to her friends with her short hair poking out under that wide hat. But she didn't look like a cabin boy, in spite of the clothes. She looked like a young woman."

14

All Is Lost

aria rushed up the back path without stopping to check on Domingo. She couldn't afford to be a minute later. A faint rustle seemed to be coming from behind the shed, but though she strained to listen, she heard only a whisper of wind. The sky was becoming cloudy and she hoped the temperature would drop.

She shifted the heavy market basket, trying to keep the handle from digging into her arm. In her free hand she clutched a slip of paper, nearly limp from the stifling humidity that gripped the air. She had to tell Rabbi Menasseh what had happened to Isobel, but that, too, would have to wait. Like the basket that weighed her down, the news that Cado had brought seemed to pull at her. She slipped off her clogs and pushed open the half-door that led to the kitchen.

The tile floor gleamed and Freeda stood at the basin, washing beer mugs. She didn't say a word, nor did she look up, but Maria was grateful for the silence. She pushed the paper into her apron pocket, quickly placed the haddock in a cooler, and began preparing the vegetables.

She was drawn from her own thoughts to the unnatural quiet of the household. There was something amiss, and she sensed it was more than her lateness in returning from market. Still, she hesitated to ask Freeda. She rinsed the pared carrots in fresh water and sliced them into a black iron pot. As she began chopping onions, she heard the master's unmistakable voice bellow from the back parlor.

"Beer, Freeda! A mug of beer, for the love of God!"

Freeda was startled at the sound of Rembrandt's call, and the mug she had just washed slipped out of her hands and fell harmlessly back into the soapy water. She reached for a clean tankard and was just filling it when Dr. Ephraim Bonus stepped into the kitchen. Now Maria was startled. What brought Dr. Bonus to the house?

"Better fill two of those, Freeda, and let me have them."

"Yes, sir," Freeda replied, bowing her head with the false respect Maria had seen her pretend many times before. She put two filled mugs onto a small tray and handed it to the doctor.

"That's good," he said in his accented Dutch. "Just give me a little time alone with Rembrandt, if you please."

She wanted to tell him of her encounter with Cado but forced herself to hold back. Clearly, this was not the time to burden him with her concerns.

Maria and Freeda watched the trim figure recede down the hall, and exchanged glances. Maria looked questioningly at the housekeeper, but she only turned back to her washing. Maria noticed Freeda had been scrubbing the same beer mug since she had come home.

Without looking up, Freeda now taunted her with her news. "The mistress is ill," she announced gravely.

Maria felt a rising sense of alarm. Hendrickje shouldn't have gone out this morning, she thought. Had something happened to the baby? Or was Hendrickje suffering from the influenza that had felled so many of Amsterdam's citizens? She waited for a few moments, but Freeda was obviously not going to offer any information without forcing her to ask.

"What's the matter?" she prodded. "Is it from the heat?"

The girl pursed her thick lips and stared at Maria while water dripped from the mug back into the basin. "She's had a serious shock," she said, enunciating each word slowly, and speaking a bit too loudly, as if Maria were deaf or too stupid to understand. Then she turned her back.

There must have been bad news in the letter that had come this morning. Perhaps a death in her family. But why wouldn't she have told Rembrandt? I remember distinctly that Hendrickje said it was nothing of importance.

She heard the master shouting in the parlor, but his words were slurred and she couldn't understand him. She didn't hear Dr. Bonus make a response, and guessed he must be talking to his friend in soft tones or, perhaps, saying nothing at all.

Freeda finally rinsed the beer mug and stood next to Maria, wiping it slowly and waiting for the next question. As much as I want to know what has happened, I am tired of playing her game of cat and mouse. She ignored the girl and began scraping the onions into the pot. She brought a large bowl of potatoes from the pantry and began peeling them silently.

It was too much for Freeda. She seemed to feel she was losing her advantage and looked up expectantly. But Maria held her tongue. Finally, the girl could no longer tolerate the uneasy silence between them.

"The letter that came this morning was from the church elders," she announced. "They demanded that Hendrickje appear before them today." There was a definite note of superiority in her voice.

"Why would they need to see her so urgently?" Maria asked. "She will likely be in church on Sunday."

Freeda let out a critical laugh that sounded more like a snort. "She's stopped going to church, or hadn't you noticed?"

"Of course, it's getting difficult for Hendrickje to get about, especially in this heat. The coming baby weighs her down more each day. Why would the elders make her walk all that way?"

Freeda lowered her voice, as if she was sharing a confidence. "They called her in to confess. That's what happens to those who disregard the church's teachings and flaunt their sins for all to see."

Maria was confused. "What sins could Hendrickje have to confess?"

Freeda became impatient and fairly hissed at her. "Are you so innocent you can't see what's staring you plainly in the face? Hendrickje was called before the elders to confess she's living in sin with the master and bearing his child without the blessing of matrimony. She had to beg forgiveness for her sins or be banned from the church. It was too much for her to handle alone, but if she'd brought the master along, he would have insulted the elders and made things worse."

Maria was stunned. She couldn't believe that Rembrandt and Hendrickje were not man and wife in the eyes of everyone, including the church. I've seen her love for the master and Titus, and their feelings for her. And yet, she realized, Titus never called Hendrickje "Mother." And Hendrickje frequently kept to her room when wealthy patrons called upon Rembrandt to choose a painting for their homes. Surely it was only that she didn't wish to interfere in Rembrandt's business dealings. Or was she keeping herself out of the public eye for fear of criticism?

"Why, she was nothing but a kitchen maid, just like us!" Freeda barked, but her accusations stopped abruptly when Titus burst into the room.

"What are you doing standing about?" he scolded Freeda, and her face turned white. "Fix some tea for Hendrickje and I shall carry it up. Just because we're busy tending to her doesn't mean the rest of the household should come to a halt. There's still a houseful needing dinner." Maria kept peeling potatoes while Freeda brewed tea in a small brown pot. There was an angry shout from Rembrandt in the parlor and the sound of his fist banging into the wall. They all plainly heard him but tried to ignore his fury, hoping Dr. Bonus would calm him down.

Maria had heard the master rail against the church and its rules before. Titus said his father believed strongly in the Bible but hated the church's rigid ways. It annoyed Rembrandt that Hendrickje took her faith so seriously. Maria guessed he would be furious at the humiliation Hendrickje had been subjected to today, and the fact that it had made her ill would be a further source of his anger. Maria peeled faster, and watched Titus carry the teapot and a thick mug back upstairs.

She was just cutting the last of the potatoes into the pot when Dr. Bonus returned. There was silence from the parlor.

"Rembrandt is resting now," he announced, "but I'll need one of you girls to mop up some spilled beer, I'm afraid."

Maria picked up a mop and a rag and followed Dr. Bonus back down the hallway. "Dr. Bonus, is Hendrickje going to be all right?" she inquired.

The doctor stopped and patted her shoulder. "It has been a very difficult day, and she's suffering from heat exhaustion. I'm as worried about the baby as I am about her, but I believe she will recover with complete rest. Can you and Freeda manage the household together? Rembrandt is not going to be of much help for a while."

Maria reassured him, although she was not sure how she would work with Freeda without Hendrickje to designate the tasks. She fingered the paper Cado had given her. She couldn't hold back any longer.

"Dr. Bonus," she said, "I've had some news today as well. I wonder if I might trouble you with it."

The doctor stroked his pointed beard and leaned forward attentively. "Today the missing ship from Recife came into the harbor." Dr. Bonus's gray-tipped eyebrows lifted with interest. "I met the cook, and he told me that my sister Isobel was on that ship. During the voyage, it was attacked by Spanish privateers and she and several other Jewish passengers were captured."

Her voice rose with concern. "They were to be sold to the Inquisition for ransom."

"God forbid!" breathed the doctor.

The full impact of Cado's news seemed to hit Maria for the first time. "My sister is gone," she blurted out.

Dr. Bonus looked at her solemnly. "I won't tell you the news isn't frightening, but there have been times when the congregation has ransomed others from the same fate. It's a matter of finding the privateers and offering them more money than the Inquisition. In fact, occasionally the church has been known to contact us and make an offer of freedom."

Maria held out the names Cado had given her with a trembling hand. She pointed to the first name on the list. "This is the cook," she said. "He's called Cado, and he's staying aboard *The Valck* while it's here for repairs. He knew Isobel and can explain what happened. The second name is the name of the captain of the ship. Cado says he can be reached through the East India Company here in Amsterdam." She tried to think of the future. "What else can I do?"

"Right now you can only wait. I'm going to check on Hendrickje once more before I leave, then I shall go directly to Rabbi Menasseh's and tell him the news. Don't give up hope."

Maria walked quietly into the parlor, where Rembrandt was resting in a chair by the window. The drapes were pulled closed to keep out the sun, and the still air reeked of beer and sweat.

She tiptoed over and saw the spilled beer that stained his loose shirt and lay in a frothy puddle near his propped feet. She ran the mop across the tiles, absorbing what she could, and went outside to the well to rinse it with clear water. She looked at the shed longingly, wishing she could visit Domingo. If only she could hold him for just a minute. Surely, he would need fresh water in this heat, but she left the mop to dry against the shed and reluctantly returned to finish cleaning with the washrag.

The master stirred when she entered and opened his eyes a bit. "All is lost," he muttered. Maria realized he was drunk. She bent down to wipe the floor, but he reached out and gripped her arm. He leaned toward her and fixed his reddened eyes on her face, with no sign of recognition.

"Who are they to tell us how to live?" he grumbled. "Hypocrites!" he fairly spat, and she turned her face from the smell of his beery breath. Then he dropped her arm and settled into a half-sleep, and Maria thought she saw tears fill the edges of his closed eyes. She finished wiping the floor and heard him mumble, "All is lost," just as she slipped out the door.

She rinsed the rag and hung it to dry on the empty clothesline. Rembrandt's frightening pronouncement reflected her deepest fears. She felt drained of all energy and, like the master, nearly empty of hope. Was he afraid the baby would be lost, or Hendrickje? Or perhaps he meant the house. Titus had told her that they owed a large sum and that Heer Thyss, the man who had sold it to them, wanted his payment in full. If Rembrandt couldn't pay off the debt soon, the city would auction off their belongings until the amount was raised. She thought of the rooms full of paintings and drawings, vases and statues, all surely worth a huge sum. Rembrandt had loaded every space with collections of rare and exotic things. But without them, the house would be barren. Those possessions reflected their owner.

Maria glanced toward the kitchen to see if Freeda was watching her. She needed just a few minutes with Domingo and had learned from the lazy girl how to steal some time alone. She filled the watering can at the well. If anyone is watching, they'll think I'm watering the garden. But she turned instead to the shed.

Domingo would need fresh water. She entered the wooden structure and realized that it was actually cooler than the air outdoors. She looked around, clicking her tongue, but Domingo did not come forward. Unfamiliar footprints were pressed faintly into the dirt and Domingo's basket was turned sideways. She straightened his empty apple crate and called him. "Domingo!"

She tossed out the stale water in his dish and refilled it with fresh water from the watering can. Then she took two pieces of carrot that she had saved and added them to his food supply. The lettuce she had given him this morning was still in his dish, wilted and pale, and a slice of apple, his favorite, lay dried and brown. Maybe he's lost his appetite in this heat, she thought. She looked behind the rake and the hoe, checked into shadowy corners and empty flowerpots, but she couldn't find him anywhere. He always runs up when I come in. Where could he be?

"Domingo?" Maria called, and as her voice echoed back she heard a note of fear. The door was latched and no one ever comes in here. Especially today, with all the commotion of Hendrickje rushing out and then coming home ill. And someone must have hurried out to find Dr. Bonus.

She tried to think through the possibilities. Perhaps Domingo was just hiding. She went out with the watering can and latched the door. I'll water the vegetables, she decided. When I come back, he's bound to be lapping the water with his pink little tongue or nibbling at the carrots. He has to be inside the shed somewhere.

She watched the sprinkle of water darken the parched ground. A thick breeze stirred the air. Maria looked up to see gray clouds rolling in from the ocean. In the distance she heard the faint sound of thunder. Rain is what we all need, she thought. It would clear the air.

But where could Domingo be? He wouldn't leave the shed unless someone carried him. Anything not to step on the grass! She shook the last drops from the watering can and walked back to the shed. This time she rattled the door and stomped heavily across the dirt floor. She couldn't help but notice that the imprint of her clogs did not match the larger prints beside them. Maria's heart beat faster.

She stepped out of the shed, leaving the door open, and looked nervously around the yard. If he has gotten out, I'll just have to calm down and find him. She stood near the steps to the attic studio and paced herself across the length of the yard. Up and down she walked, taking small careful steps and looking around closely. When she came to a flower bed, or any spot where he might be hidden, she called softly, "Domingo! Where are you, little friend?"

At the edge of the compost heap Maria noticed a barrel-shaped wooden button resting in the grass. A few frayed threads were still attached to the holes that had fastened it. She slipped the curious object into her dress pocket.

Then her eye caught a pale yellow tint contrasting with the dull brown of the compost. She stepped closer. It was a wedge of cheese, sprinkled with dots of white. The rough edges on it had obviously been chewed, perhaps by a small animal. Was it moldy cheese someone had thrown out? Titus said they used the decomposing pile only for weeds and grass.

Maria bent down and reached for the cheese to examine it more closely but stopped before she touched it. It was not moldy but instead had a powdery substance sprinkled on it. Suddenly she stood up in horror. Rat poison!

Images of the gaunt, crooked-toothed rat catcher she had seen the first morning in the marketplace haunted her. She remembered his cold, frightening gaze and the dead rats that dangled from a stick over his shoulder.

"Domingo!" she cried out, her throat tight and dry. "Domingo!"

A clay flowerpot lay at the back of the compost heap, its chipped saucer discarded on the ground nearby. Maria recognized the pot from the shed and saw the faint traces of chalk Titus had used to write its Dutch name for her. Who had moved it? A peal of thunder roared overhead and a few large drops of rain began to splash onto the ground, but she did not turn to go in. She saw a tiny pink paw sticking out of the mounded weeds. With her fingers, she dug away the layers until she was staring at the elongated shape of brown and white fur. Maria's eyes filled with tears as the clouds opened and sent sheets of rain across the parched yard.

She leaned forward, trying to focus on the blurred shape. Domingo lay stiff, his eyes closed and a thin line of sickening white foam lining his open mouth. Maria's entire body shook with sobs as rain pelted her from above. Her wet hair clung to her face, and her dress was soaked and heavy.

She turned and ran blindly into the house, her clothes dripping on the clean tiled floor. Freeda shouted at her, but the words fell away from Maria like the water on her dress. She raced through the hallway and up the stairs, not knowing where she was going until she ran into Titus standing in confusion on the landing. Without knowing what had caused her tears, he reached for her and enfolded her in his arms.

15

Making a Splash

I lined a salt box with straw," Titus said quietly, "and nailed down the lid to be sure no cat could get at him."

Maria didn't move her head but continued to stare straight ahead. "I heard you hammering in the shed. I'm grateful, Titus. I couldn't do it myself. I really couldn't."

"I know." Titus paused, his eyes on Maria. "I buried him next to the garden. I thought that would be the perfect place for him because he loved playing between the vegetables."

A sad smile played across her lips as she remembered Domingo scampering among the plants. It was right to remember, even though it pained her.

"Sit perfectly still!" Rembrandt scolded, but there was no anger in his command. "You are disturbing my model, Titus. You know better than to bother me while I'm working."

Maria had been posing in Rembrandt's studio for a new painting. He had seated her on a simple wooden chair and placed an open letter in her hands. A sewing basket rested on the floor beside her. The master in-

structed her to gaze out the window as if she were absorbed in thought about the news the letter contained.
It was easy to enact his scenario. If only I were reading
a real letter. One from my parents or Isobel.

Rembrandt daubed his brush into a thick puddle of
blue paint on his palette and squinted at the blue shawl
that was draped over her shoulders. He lightly stroked
the paint onto the canvas before him.

"But Father, dinner is waiting, and so are a tableful
of starving apprentices."

Rembrandt blinked, as if coming out of a trance. "Is
it dinnertime again? Or have my pupils simply remained at the table since yesterday? It seems we do
nothing but feed those rascals." He picked up a brush
with thin bristles and rolled it through a bead of gray-
white paint. "They don't pay enough for their keep,
let alone their lessons." He let out a deep grunt as he
made a delicate highlight on the folds of the shawl.
"What does it matter, now? I'll be lucky to keep a roof
over their work if Thyss doesn't give me more time."

Maria had noticed that the master went about his
work with little hint of the despair he had shown yesterday, except for a trace of redness in his eyes. She
blamed his frightening mood on the shock of Hendrickje's reprimand from the church and the effects of
too much to drink.

"Come on, Father, you know how grumpy Freeda
gets when the dinner goes cold."

"Freeda! She's grumpy all the time, except when her
mouth is full!" Rembrandt wiped the excess paint from
his brush onto his already stained smock and set his
palette onto the small table that held oils, tinted pow-
ders, and small jars of mixed colors. That was the sig-

nal Maria had learned to welcome. She rubbed her stiff shoulders and stood up. "Is it so much work for the model?" Rembrandt teased. "Just to sit still for a few hours? What of the poor painter who stands on his feet and must show something for his time?"

"Go along, Father." Titus laughed, taking the shawl from Maria and draping it over a thronelike chair heaped with lengths of brocade fabric and velvet cloth. "We'll put things right here."

"What, will you miss Freeda's hotpot? I could smell the beef boiling all the way up here." For a moment he looked a bit guilty. "I know the meat was an extravagance, Titus, but it will help Hendrickje regain her strength. She needs to eat well."

"I think Maria needs to get out for a bit. I thought we could take some of the etchings to a dealer for you. Then perhaps we'll treat ourselves to a pancake at the market."

Maria wanted to sample the thick, sugary pancake just once, but she would refuse to patronize the woman who had chased her off that first day. There were other sellers flipping the hotcakes in their long-handled pans. Then she remembered Hendrickje.

"I should stay and help," she offered. "Even if Hendrickje is feeling better today, she should be resting. I can't just go off and leave her."

Rembrandt opened a thick portfolio and brought out a loose pile of etchings. "She'll be fine," he reassured her as he laid them out. "Hendrickje was feeling much stronger this morning. Thank goodness for the storm that swept through yesterday. The change in the air has certainly helped her recovery. Come, Titus, help me count these."

Each square etching was signed with Rembrandt's signature and bore two numbers in the lower left-hand corner. "Shall I stop at one hundred?" Titus asked.

Maria looked over Titus's shoulder. It was strange to see her own face looking back at her from the drawings. So many Marias, all looking steadily forward. It was harder to see her face captured by Rembrandt's pen than to look into a mirror. She could always change her reflection in the glass by moving or turning away. But the face in the etching would never change. "What do the numbers mean?" she asked. "Why are there two?"

"The first number tells in what order the print was made and the second tells how many prints in all," Titus said. "So if the number says 10/250, it means it's the tenth print made in a run of 250 etchings."

"It tells what they're worth," Rembrandt declared. "The early prints are usually too light. Then the press starts working better and the ink covers the copper plate just right. The ones in the middle are the best. The last ones begin to blur a bit. Sometimes there's too much ink." He looked at Titus's growing pile. "Take the middle fifty," he advised, "and bring them to van Dyke over on Kalverstraat. His shop is always busy and I think he'll sell them quicker. Tell him I won't take less than thirty guilders each."

Titus stopped his counting and checked through the piles he was forming. "There seem to be two missing," he frowned. "Everything was in order through 148, but the next number is 151."

The master searched the empty portfolio and then shuffled through a bin of loose sketches. "I numbered these myself. I know I'm sometimes distracted, but I'm sure I didn't skip numbers." He looked exasperated. "I seem to be losing things every day." He glanced around the studio with a tired look. "You know my Chinese bowl? The one with the blue lion painted on the bottom? I wanted to use it in a still life I was setting up for the students, and I couldn't find it. I don't know what I did with it."

"It has to be here somewhere," Titus said. "We really ought to straighten up this studio. There's no telling what we'd find. For now, we'll take the middle forty-eight etchings to van Dyke."

Rembrandt rested a hand on Titus's shoulder for a moment. "Go ahead, you two, and take your time." Down the stairs he ambled, his paint-smeared smock still on and the pungent smell of linseed oil following him out.

Titus wiped the excess paint from the brushes with a rag, while Maria filled a glazed jar with turpentine. She took the brushes and swished them around in the cleansing fluid.

"Who could have poisoned Domingo?" she asked, and then answered her own question. "I think it must have been Freeda."

"We don't know that," Titus cautioned.

"But Domingo was so tame," she argued. "He wasn't afraid of people." Her voice caught in her throat. "Whoever did it must have lured him into the flowerpot with the poisoned cheese and then trapped him inside by dropping the saucer on top. You know he wouldn't have walked across the grass to the compost pile himself." Titus had to agree.

"Freeda must have caught him when I left for market. There's no one else. You were with your friends.

Rembrandt was printing etchings with the apprentices, and Hendrickje was at the church." Maria looked down at the dripping brushes. She had not meant to refer to Hendrickje's reprimand and couldn't meet Titus's eyes.

"It's all right," he reassured her. "You don't need to be ashamed for us."

"I'm not!" she declared. "I have nothing but admiration for Hendrickje."

"If only the church elders could share your view," he complained. "Father would have married her long ago, except for my mother's will."

Maria didn't want to pry into the family's private affairs, so she held back her questions. But Titus seemed eager to explain.

"My mother, Saskia, left her family inheritance to me when she died, and gave Father the legal right to draw on that money until I became an adult. It's income we depend upon. In spite of his fame, Father's paintings don't bring in enough money to provide for us all the time. Sometimes he is flooded with buyers, but then there are long stretches when his work is simply out of favor. And truthfully, he's never understood how to hold back in lean times. He just keeps spending, waiting for the money he expects to earn in the future."

Maria didn't see how Rembrandt's shortsighted spending had anything to do with marrying Hendrickje, but she kept silent. She helped Titus open the shuttered windows so the cool breeze that had pushed out the evening's rain would freshen the air in the studio. She watched the young man fasten the shutters and thought of how much he had grown in the weeks since she had come to live with the family. From a curious, inquisitive boy filled with impatient energy, he had become more patient and watchful.

"When Saskia's will was drawn up, there was one obscure clause that said Rembrandt wouldn't be allowed to draw any money if he remarried. I don't know whether my mother intended it that way, although surely neither she nor my father could have imagined he would ever choose to marry another. It could have been a condition made by Saskia's family. Father says they never had any faith in him."

Titus wrapped the etchings to be sold in a sheet of brown paper and tied it with string. He glanced protectively around the studio, making sure everything was in order before he closed the door behind them. "So you see, Father can't marry without losing the inheritance. And we need it now more than ever. When I reach legal age, there will be no more barriers. Then Father and Hendrickje can make things right with the church elders. But now, when she needs their support, they choose to threaten and shame her." His jaw tightened. "I'll never forgive them for that."

The pair walked down the back stairs and Titus took her hand and led her toward the vegetable garden. A small circle of stones marked the patch of earth where he had buried Domingo. Maria thought of her pet's soft pink tongue and his tiny ears. She remembered the way he had pulled playfully at her hair. There were no words she could speak without letting her emotions overcome her. She gave Titus's hand a squeeze.

As they walked up the Breestraat, Maria looked toward Rabbi Menasseh's house. "I wonder if I should stop and ask the rabbi if he's heard anything about Isobel?"

Titus linked his arm with hers without slowing his pace. "It was only yesterday that Dr. Bonus passed along your news," he reminded her. "I'm sure he'll tell you as soon as he learns anything. Now, no more worrying for at least two hours."

Maria relaxed against his arm. Through her sorrow over Domingo, she had found comfort with Titus. He had consoled her yesterday when she first discovered her pet in the compost pile, and he had sensed when it was best to talk and when she simply needed to cry.

She breathed deeply, savoring the cool air. "I keep telling myself that perhaps Domingo wouldn't have survived on the ship if I hadn't taken care of him," she said. "But it doesn't make me feel any better."

"From what my father told me, I would say you saved him twice—once on the ship and then again in the marketplace. Those farm wives are quite good with a broom!" Titus stopped as they crossed the second bridge and looked down into the rippling water. "You gave Domingo something more than just a chance to live," he said seriously. "Living isn't always enough. He learned to trust you, and that is a much greater gift."

A small pebble rolled off the arched side of the bridge and sent out a series of silent ripples. Maria watched them reach out in ever-widening circles until they faded into nothingness.

"Isobel trusted me, too," she said, "and I failed her." She pushed another small stone into the water below. "Do you see how the rings in the water reach out farther and farther until they disappear?" Titus nodded

solemnly. "That is the picture of my life. I keep reaching out, to Domingo, to Isobel, for my parents. But
even though I start out with a splash, nothing comes
of my efforts. They fade away as if I never tried." A
flat-bottomed barge sailed under the bridge. The boat-
man looked up and raised his arm in silent greeting.
Titus lifted his cap and held it in the air a moment as
the boat proceeded on its journey.

"If you threw in a bigger stone," Titus smiled, "the
ripples would be felt a long way, and some of them
would reach all the way to shore. Maybe you just need
to make a bigger splash."

16

A New Address

itus pushed open the door at van Dyke's and a small bell tinkled overhead. Its sunny window faced the busy street where smartly dressed couples stopped to admire the display of paintings and china. Maria was impressed with the wide array of portraits and landscapes that lined the walls, but she sensed that Rembrandt's works were more important. Many of the canvases in van Dyke's gallery featured a thin wash of paint, unlike the thick strokes on the master's pieces. The gallery drawings seemed to lack the vitality that made Rembrandt's subjects come alive for her.

A short, impeccably dressed man emerged from a back room. He extended a hand to Titus.

"Why, young van Rijn!" He eyed the small package sharply. "What have you brought me today?"

"Good afternoon, Heer van Dyke," Titus greeted him. "Have you met our guest, Maria Ben Lazar?"

Van Dyke gave a short bow and gestured to two tall chairs with gold silk cushions. "Please sit down."

Titus settled into the chair as if he were an experienced businessman and Maria sat quietly observing him. He placed the unopened package in his lap.

"Father has been quite busy lately," he began. "What with his commissions and portraits and such. But he has struck a new etching."

Heer van Dyke frowned and his fingers twitched in his lap. "I do hope it's nothing quite as tawdry as the last one. It's not easy to sell pictures of a street drunkard, no matter how fine the execution."

Titus began unknotting the twine, and van Dyke pulled a silk handkerchief from his breast pocket and wiped his hands nervously, as if they had to be dust-free before handling the etchings.

"I think you'll be pleased with these," Titus reassured him, and unwrapped the paper. He placed the packet of drawings into the dealer's eager hands. Van Dyke took one look at them and his eyebrows lifted in surprise. Then he fixed his small gray eyes on Maria's face.

"Exceptional," he declared. "A fitting tribute to the beauty of the subject." Maria dropped her eyes and felt her face growing warm. She should have waited for Titus outside. It didn't seem proper for the etchings to be judged in front of their model.

Van Dyke unobtrusively checked to be sure the prints were signed by the master. "I can get thirty guilders for each one, I'm certain."

That was just what Rembrandt had asked, but Titus gracefully lifted the packet of etchings back onto the brown wrapping. "I'm afraid that wouldn't do," he said. There was a long moment of silence, which made Maria uncomfortable, but which Titus seemed to relish.

Heer van Dyke locked his fingers together tightly. "These are not the best of times," he advised. "Markets have fallen and even Amsterdam's best families are feeling the pinch. And though my commission is modest, I must cover my own expenses." Titus began to wrap the etchings.

Van Dyke sighed. "What would the master like to obtain?"

"Fifty guilders each," Titus said. Maria tried not to show her surprise.

The dealer rose to his feet. "Impossible! It would take me months to sell them at that price."

Titus began to tie the string around the package, and Maria wondered what he would do with the etchings now. Van Dyke paced to the window and back. He stood in front of Titus, and Maria noticed that Rembrandt's son was nearly taller than the man, even though he was still seated. He didn't look up but patiently continued tying the string.

"Forty guilders is the best I can do," van Dyke offered, raising his voice. "And even then, I'll have to look for foreign buyers."

"Ask fifty, then," Titus said calmly. Van Dyke reached for the package and unwrapped it. He spread the etchings on a polished mahogany table and studied them carefully. "Have you given me just the middle run?" he asked.

"Certainly," Titus said, walking over to the dealer. "There are forty-eight there. When you've sold these, we can give you the end runs for less."

Van Dyke shook Titus's hand. "Fifty guilders, then," he said. "But you'll need to give me a little time. I'm sure your father sends you here because you are such a shrewd bargainer."

Titus laughed. "You know the people who are wait-

ing for my father's work, Herr van Dyke." Titus smiled.
"I expect to see these sold in no time at all."

The dealer smiled at Maria. "Tell that crusty Rembrandt I can sell anything he paints as long as it's a picture of you."

Titus took Maria's arm and drew her along the busy street. "I'm starving," he announced. She could hear the playful note that defined Titus the first day she had met him. "Where shall we go? Should we head to the market and walk around while we eat? Or should we stop in a pancake house and sit like a proper lady and gentleman?" But before he could make up his mind or wait for her opinion, he was distracted by a small crowd of people gathered just ahead.

A curious group of passersby stood in a ragged semi-circle in front of a narrow brick house. A pair of wide windows had been thrown open on the third level, and all eyes were riveted toward them. A workman in baggy blue pants and a loose smock shouted above the din of chatter around him.

"Dirk! Lower the rope!"

Titus pulled Maria toward the front of the gathering. "They're moving something!" he said with excitement. "See the pulley?"

She scanned her eyes to the peak of the tall building and saw that a pulley had been attached to the iron hook she had observed in nearly every roof peak in Amsterdam. A length of rope dangled from the contraption, and both ends of it disappeared into the open windows high above.

"What are they doing?"

Titus seemed astonished by Maria's ignorance. "Haven't you seen anyone moving since you've been here?" But, true to his old habits, he didn't wait for an answer. "Surely you didn't think people could move furniture up the winding, narrow staircases in these houses, did you? That's why we've got such wide windows! And roof hooks for the pulleys! Watch!" He drew Maria in front of him, and she was again aware of how much taller Titus was even though she was older.

A second workman led a horse-drawn open wagon through the growing crowd of onlookers. A massive, carved wooden wardrobe stood imposingly in the back. There was a loud whistle from above, and a thick rope dropped. A young man standing in the crowd stepped forward and held the horse's halter, while the two workmen began draping the wardrobe in heavy blankets and tying it up like a package. Finally, the pulley rope was knotted securely.

"Ho! Dirk!" shouted the first worker. "Heave to!"

The men standing in the wagon guided the heavy piece, and before Maria's astonished eyes the wardrobe began to wobble and then rise into the air. Whistles and cheers rose from the crowd. The people pulled back into a wider circle, laughing nervously as it swung dangerously overhead. A few young boys pushed each other toward the open space, and one made a dash from one side to the other, drawing admiring approval from his friends.

In a moment the two workmen reappeared at the upper window, one lending his hands to pull and the other leaning precariously out to steady the swinging wardrobe so that it wouldn't crash into the house. A collective gasp arose as he reached for the rope and missed. Higher and higher the sturdy piece rose, as if it were destined for the rooftop.

"This is crazy," Maria whispered. "What happens if they can't hold it?"

"It crashes!" Titus said with enthusiasm. "It's spectacular!"

"Heave! Heave!" shouted the workmen in unison, and the crowd fell silent. With one quick grab, the man leaning from the window reached the rope and pulled the swinging wardrobe toward him. It bumped against the window frame and was then eased into the unseen room above. The crowd stamped its feet and let out an approving cheer. Boys put their fingers to their mouths and let out shrill whistles. Maria would never again wonder what roof hooks were for, but she would never understand houses that were so narrow a person couldn't move his furniture up the stairs. Rembrandt wouldn't need such a dangerous ritual in his wide house. So long as he kept it.

The sound of clopping shoes alerted her that the Lady in Red was not far behind. She turned to see that today the woman, huffing and puffing up the street, was the Lady in Green. Maria tugged at Titus's sleeve. When he saw the woman hurriedly approaching, he gave a soft groan under his breath.

"Titus! Maria!" she called, and several people in the departing crowd stared at the flushed woman, rustling her skirts as she approached.

She patted her chest in a fluttering motion and panted as if she had been running for miles. "Rembrandt told me you had gone to van Dyke's, and I've been trying to catch up with you ever since. Thank goodness you stopped. I thought I'd never find you."

"What did you want with us?" Titus asked, and this time he waited for an answer.

Dame Prinsenhof tugged open a green fabric purse that dangled from her arm and rummaged about. "Not you, Titus," she said with exasperation. "Maria. Now, where is it?"

She continued fumbling in her bag, pulling out wrinkled handkerchiefs and unmatched gloves before she finally sighed with relief. "Ah, here it is." She smoothed a crumpled piece of paper and held it out toward Maria. "The name isn't Ben Lazar, but it's worth looking into." She grasped one string of her purse in each hand and choked it shut. Then she straightened her green hat and trotted off, her slippers clattering against the cobblestones.

Maria showed Titus the name and address that were scrawled across the paper. "Willem van Licht, 57 Oud-estraat."

"That's in the district where they sell antiques," Titus declared. "It's not far at all. We could find it now, if you want."

"But what about your pancake?" she asked. "You said you were starving."

"I can wait. This might be important."

"She didn't even say who we were finding," Maria said. "Maybe it's someone with news. But it's a Dutch name, not a Jewish one."

"And it's not in the Jewish quarter," Titus added.

"Perhaps it's someone from the East India Company. Maybe he has news about Isobel." She began to feel hopeful that the name on the paper in her hand held promise. "Can you help me find the house?"

Without a word, Titus took her arm and turned toward the canal they had just crossed. They walked in silence, but she felt they shared an understanding that did not need words.

They walked quickly through twisted, narrow streets past shops crammed with dusty urns and tattered furniture. Instead of the open windows on street level where housewives sat and sewed, she saw storefront windows filled with musty collections of treasures from days long past. Titus suddenly stopped short. He looked at the paper she held and gestured toward a narrow black door displaying 57 in brass numerals.

"Do you want me to find out who it is?" he offered.

Maria shook her head. This was something she wanted to pursue herself.

"But are you prepared if nothing comes of talking to this Heer van Licht?"

Maria never thought there could be so many disappointments in her life. "Maybe I already expect that," she said. "But I must hold out some hope, or I wouldn't have come at all." She smiled. "Maybe this time I'll make a bigger splash."

While Titus watched from the sidewalk, Maria climbed the front steps and stood in front of the shiny black door. She could see her own reflection as she lifted the heavy brass knocker and gave it three sharp raps.

17

One Perfect Shell

stocky, gray-haired woman opened the heavy door and greeted Maria in Portuguese.

"*Bem-vindo!*" she cried, "Welcome!" It seemed to Maria as if the housekeeper had been expecting her.

"I have come to see Heer van Licht," Maria announced.

The woman beckoned to Titus, who watched intently from the foot of the stairs. "*Entre!*"

Maria clasped Titus's hand as they stepped into the narrow front hallway. The housekeeper led them into a small parlor filled with richly upholstered furnishings. Heavy tapestry drapes covered the windows and blocked all but the thinnest rays of sunshine from entering the cool, dim room.

Maria and Titus sank into the deep cushions of a small sofa and sat stiffly.

"The master and mistress will be with you in a moment," the woman said, folding her hands over her crisply starched apron. "Make yourselves comfortable and I will bring you some refreshment."

"Please don't go to any trouble," Titus protested. "We've only come to speak to Heer van Licht for a moment." But the woman merely smiled and left the room.

"It's odd for an Amsterdam gentleman to have a Portuguese servant," Titus whispered. "And look at this room! These things are not bought in the market. They're imported from the East." Maria shuffled her feet on the thick carpet. It had dark tones of burgundy with swirling patterns in rose and deep blue. It seemed too fine to cover a floor, and she could imagine it adorning the wall of a castle.

The servant returned and set a tray of delicate pink-patterned teacups and a steaming teapot on a carved wooden sideboard, between two silver candlesticks. When she left, Maria slipped to the buffet and inhaled the sweet aroma.

"It's rosewater tea," she said. "The van Lichts have a taste for Portuguese food." She looked at the candlesticks more closely in the dim light. Why did they draw her? She ran her finger lightly around the cold ring of tiny flowers that adorned the bowl of the candlestick but pulled her hand away when the servant returned to place a tray of sweets on the low table in front of the sofa.

"Look at those!" Titus marveled when the woman had gone. "I think this is our dinner. How many do you think I can eat before someone comes in?" He reached for a curiously twisted biscuit, topped with a sprinkling of sesame seeds.

"*Biscochos!*" Maria exclaimed. He stopped in midbite, looking at her questioningly. "Those are called *biscochos*," she explained, her voice shaking with emotion. "I made those with my mother hundreds of times. I remember twisting ropes of dough to give it that special shape."

Realizing that the biscuit was safe to eat, Titus popped it into his mouth. "Delicious!" he mumbled, his cheeks bulging as he chewed.

Maria sat close to him. "I'm afraid." Her voice was shaky. "Something is happening here. I don't know what it is, but it's scaring me." Her throat felt tight and dry. She stood up nervously, as if ready to run out of the house.

Before she could take a step, the van Lichts walked into the salon. Maria froze, and Titus gulped down the last piece of biscuit. He rose to greet the couple. Heer van Licht was a tall, clean-shaven man dressed in a gray suit with a flat white collar. A shiny bald spot gleamed at his forehead, and thin gray locks fell just below his ears. His wife was slender as a reed and nearly as tall as her husband. She wore a blue linen dress with a ruffle of lace at the neck and wrists. Her hair was pure white. It was pulled back smoothly from her face and fastened into a neat bun. On her ears, tiny pearls hung from delicate gold wires.

Titus cleared his throat and tried to break the awkward silence that enveloped the room. "I am Titus van Rijn, and this is Maria Ben Lazar. We were told that you might have information about Maria's family."

Heer van Licht's eyes lingered on Maria's face while he held his hands behind him. Maria felt dazed and unable to think clearly. The woman's almond-shaped face and round, heavy-lidded eyes evoked memories she could not define, and the man's stately bearing reminded her of a sheltering figure from a long-ago time.

Titus shifted his feet and looked anxiously at the others, waiting for a response.

"Do you recognize this, Maria Serena?" asked Heer van Licht, and he held a pink conch shell on his open palms.

Maria caught her breath and felt her eyes sting with salty tears. "My shell!" she said, so softly that her voice was barely audible. "And you know my middle name. I didn't tell it to anyone." Through the tears that filled her eyes, and the sobs that began to shake her shoulders, Maria understood what she had only sensed a moment before. She reached for the couple in front of her.

"Papa? Mama?"

The man and woman began to weep as they embraced her. "My child, my daughter," sobbed the woman, rubbing her hand soothingly on Maria's back.

Titus was as shocked as Maria, but it was not his reunion. He stood in awkward silence until the joy of the moment drew him in. He grinned broadly, plopped back comfortably on the sofa, and reached for a small almond cake. As Maria and her parents tried to calm themselves and grasp the reality of having found each other, he smiled and munched, sampling each variety of sweet on the tray.

"I have traveled the world looking for my daughters," her father said, "but I never expected to find you in Amsterdam." He stepped back, wiping his eyes with a handkerchief.

"But your name," Maria protested. "Why did you deceive me with a false name? I would have found you weeks ago, but no one knew Abraham Ben Lazar."

"Sit close to me, child," her mother said, drawing

her down on a tufted bench. "There is so much to tell, so many years to relive."

"So many years when we were pushed between hope and despair," her father added. "A time when we had to hide ourselves from the long arm of the king of Portugal."

The housekeeper entered and silently poured tea. Maria's mother sipped hers as if it held a source of strength she desperately needed, but Maria's hands shook so that she could barely hold the cup. She looked searchingly at Titus.

"Did you know we would find my parents here?"

"I take no blame for this at all." He laughed. "I think we should heap all the responsibility on Dame Prinsenhof. This is her doing, isn't it?"

Eva Ben Lazar slipped her arm around her daughter's shoulders. "And what a shocking lady she is!" she remarked. "We could only expect that she would be full of surprises."

Maria's father looked serious. "Very few people know how often she helps members of the Jewish community. Dame Prinsenhof has served as a reliable contact between the *conversos* who still remain in Spain and Portugal and those of us here. It never appears suspicious when she stops to talk to a sailor whose boat has just come into port, but usually she is delivering or receiving a message. Sometimes she helps arrange the resettlement of someone who wishes to escape their life of secrecy and live openly as Jews. She helped us, and she is more than a friend."

"But I met her weeks ago," Maria exclaimed, "and she said she knew no one with the name Ben Lazar. I don't understand any of this!"

"She didn't want to betray my identity until she was certain you were my daughter. Also, I was away on business, and she didn't want your mother to face this alone. Dame Prinsenhof waited for my return and spoke to me only yesterday." Maria looked perplexed.

"Perhaps I should start at the beginning," her father said. "Titus, you'd better have another biscuit." Titus reached for another sweet and sat back contentedly. "Your mother and I stayed in Lisbon only a short time after you and your sister were taken away," Abraham said. "We contacted everyone we knew who might influence the king to bring you back safely." He shook his head sadly, remembering his futile efforts. "We couldn't even discover where you had been sent. There was great danger for us, for the king would no longer receive me. Your mother and I left the house and were hidden by friends in the countryside. When all possibility of finding you was exhausted, they helped us arrange to come to Amsterdam."

"Is that why you changed your name?" Titus asked.

"There had been a great purge at the court," Abraham explained. "Anyone suspected of secretly keeping the Jewish faith was to be turned over to the Inquisition. In order to escape Lisbon, Eva and I disguised ourselves and adopted Dutch names. I even shaved my beard," he added, rubbing his smooth chin.

"I'm afraid my hair was my disguise," her mother said. "In the few days from the time you were taken away until we arranged our escape, all my hair turned white." Maria would have recognized her mother sooner if her hair had still been dark. But she said nothing. How had her parents become so old?

"We were smuggled onto a ship bound for Amsterdam. Most of our belongings were left behind, and we salvaged only a few things."

"Like my shell?" Maria asked.

Eva stroked her daughter's hair, as if regretting the change in her own. "To be honest, that isn't the same one. Your father bought it this morning from a dealer near here. It was an idea he had to see if you really were our lost Maria."

"But how could you bring enough money to start a new life?" Maria asked. "You couldn't have sold our house."

"Ah, but we did," he said. "We prepared a document giving the house and its contents to our friends. They, in turn, raised enough gold coins to ensure that we could start a new life here."

"Weren't you afraid of all those coins being discovered?" Titus asked.

Maria's father pulled a book from a shelf nearby. He handed it to Titus. As far as Maria could see, it was a Portuguese copy of the Bible. "Open it to page 236," Abraham instructed. Titus thumbed through the pages until he found the right one.

"I don't see anything," he said.

"Exactly," Maria's father agreed. He took the book and bent the pages back. Just between the binding and the middle of the page, a neatly cut stack of paper popped out, revealing a small hidden compartment. Maria and Titus laughed in astonishment. "You wouldn't expect thieves to study the Bible," he explained. "And I have quite a collection of books."

Eva continued their story. "Even after we arrived here, Abraham was afraid the king would search for him. He was one of the court's closest advisers and knew many secrets of the king's rule."

"Amsterdam has an emissary from Portugal living here, and there are many spies at his disposal," added Maria's father. "That's why we changed our name and kept away from the Jewish quarter, even from the synagogue. I couldn't take the chance of being recognized. I began working as a tobacco importer and spent much of my time traveling."

Eva poured more tea. As she stood at the sideboard, Maria realized one of the clues she had to her parents' identity. "Mama, are those the candlesticks we had in Lisbon? I think I recognize the ring of flowers."

Her mother smiled. "Do you remember all the Friday nights we whispered the blessings over the candles in those holders?" Maria nodded. "I couldn't leave those behind."

She had been dreading the moment when her parents would ask about Isobel. Her heart beat faster. She could wait no longer.

"Papa," she began, and tears choked her voice again. "I have lost Isobel."

"No," her father said. He brushed his hand against her cheek. "Isobel is lost, but not because of you. She is lost in spite of all you did. I know everything."

Maria's mother sniffled into a lace handkerchief. "We've had many disappointments over the years, but we never lost faith. Today, God brought us you. Soon He will see us find Isobel."

"I have been in contact with the captain of *The Valck*," Abraham said, "and with officials of the East India Company. They are using all the information they can gather to locate the Jews who were captured."

Maria heard the church bells toll two o'clock and jumped up. "Titus, we're expected back. Hendrickje will be needing us."

Titus stood up and licked a crumb from his finger. "You can't leave now. I'll take care of things." He shook his head sadly. "Anyway, Hendrickje will have to learn to get along without you."

Maria thought of her days in the van Rijn household. There was the pain of losing Domingo and her contempt for Freeda, but there was also the gentleness of Hendrickje, the kindness that Rembrandt had shown her, and Titus's friendship.

"I won't leave," she reassured him. "Not completely. After all, there are all those beets and carrots to be tended. And the baby coming!" She beamed at him while she grasped her mother's hand. "I can at least come during the days. After all, how will the master finish his painting if I don't sit?"

"Ah, yes." Titus chuckled as he headed for the door. He imitated his father's gruff voice. "Perr-fectly still!"

18

Confronting a Thief

hhh-choo!"

Everyone looked up at Titus's explosive sneeze, but no one said a word. Heads quickly turned back to the food in front of them. Rembrandt poked at his food with a knife. Titus watched his father warily, and the apprentices tried to eat without being noticed. Freeda reached across the table and spooned another heaping serving of potatoes onto her plate.

"This is supposed to be a celebration," Titus said, wiping his nose on his handkerchief. "Maria's portrait is finally finished, and we haven't all been together for dinner for two weeks. What's wrong, Father?"

Maria thought of Hendrickje upstairs in bed. She had been listless and dizzy the past few days and Dr. Bonus insisted she stay off her feet until the baby was born. It would only be a month before Hendrickje would become a mother, although no one would deny she had been a mother to Titus since he was a small child.

But it was not Hendrickje who occupied the master's thoughts today. He dropped his napkin onto the table and looked steadily at each of the young people seated around the table.

"Yesterday I decided to clean out the shed," he announced. Freeda began choking on a mouthful of food and reached for the pitcher of water. One of the apprentices thumped her on the back, but Rembrandt ignored her.

"With the baby coming, I thought everything should be cleaned, inside and out, and that seemed a good place to start. I thought I'd throw away all the broken pots and tools, sweep the floor, and spread a clean layer of sand. But when I moved one of the baskets, it felt quite heavy."

Rembrandt had everyone's attention. Freeda had stopped coughing and began to remove some plates from the table. "Sit down, Freeda," the master ordered, and she dropped into her chair.

"The basket looked like it held nothing but straw. Why should it feel heavy, I wondered? When I pulled out the straw, I found something I thought was lost." Rembrandt unwrapped a cloth-covered bundle that he had placed beneath his chair. He held up a white bowl looking ancient with its cracked glaze, and painted with a blue Oriental lion. "Today I have the unpleasant duty of discovering who in my household has been stealing from me." He sighed, a deep, dejected sound that announced his disappointment more clearly than words.

Titus took the bowl from his father and set it on the table. "I remember when you told me you had misplaced it. It was the day Maria and I took the etchings to van Dyke. Maybe it was just a prank. Remember the time the students painted a coin on the floor of their studio?" Titus forced a laugh. "You thought it was real, Father, and tried to pick it up." His attempt to soften the moment with humor failed.

"The bowl was clearly stolen," Rembrandt declared. "And it had to be taken by someone with access to my studio." He looked around the table with sadness in his eyes. "It could have been one of you apprentices. You're left to work independently at times each day, and you have always been welcome to borrow props." The students sat in silence. Rembrandt turned to Freeda.

"You've been told to stay out of my room, but how many times have I returned to find you meddling with my things?"

"I was only cleaning, master," Freeda protested. She hung her head and pulled nervously at her apron. "Things get dusty, all those shells and swords and statues. The mistress likes things to be tidy." Then Freeda pointed at Maria. "Maybe it was her!" she accused. "She's the one who had the run of the house. No duties to worry about, like me. Just in and out, to market, to the garden, off on a jaunt with Titus!" She fairly spat out her words. "And she's the one who was always at the shed. I wouldn't go near that filthy rat!"

Maria felt her face go hot with anger and embarrassment. She couldn't find her voice. How could Freeda accuse her of stealing? Why, the master had saved her from jail. He had taken her in and welcomed Domingo with her. He had made it possible for her to find her parents. She could never repay him for all he had done.

Titus came to her defense at once. "Maria had no reason to steal, Freeda, and you've no right to accuse her. We were caring for her until she found her family."

"I've got no parents!" Freeda shouted. "That's why I work for a living, though I get little enough to show for it."

"And there's little enough you do for what you're paid," Rembrandt chided her. "But the fact remains, someone took the bowl and hid it in the shed." He turned to Maria. "I'm not accusing you. Has there been anyone else in the shed?" She thought of the times she and Titus had taken Domingo to play in the garden, but as for other visitors, her mind was blank. She shook her head.

A loud rapping on the front door interrupted the confrontation. "I'll see who it is," Titus offered. The room fell silent, but Freeda stared smugly at Maria.

She's sure she's put the blame on me, but I'm innocent! Maria tried to think of how she could prove she hadn't taken the bowl, but knew she had to depend on the master's faith in her. If he still had any.

There was the sound of men's voices in the foyer and then boots and shoes clattering across the tiles toward the kitchen. Maria was startled to see Titus enter the kitchen with the two sheriffs who had arrested her in the marketplace the day she had arrived in Amsterdam. She rose from her seat, frightened. Would they take her to jail on Freeda's wild accusations?

But then Maria saw that sandwiched between the lawmen was the lean figure of Freeda's cousin. Although she had never seen him this close before, his shadowy form was familiar to her. At the rear of the trio was the jittery flutter of the art dealer, van Dyke.

"What's wrong?" queried a small voice. Hendrickje

squeezed uncertainly into the room. Rembrandt rushed to help her into his chair. "I heard unfamiliar voices at the door. I had to come down."

"I've caught you a thief!" van Dyke cried. He pulled two etchings from his breast pocket, and Maria saw her own image being waved in the air. "This scoundrel came into the gallery yesterday, offering me two original Rembrandts. Of course, he had no way of knowing I had just taken this very series from you. I studied them and realized that not only were they authentic but they bore the numbers 149 and 150. I had wondered why young Titus only brought me 48 copies. It was an odd number, and I hadn't stopped thinking about it. I told this rascal I'd need time to determine a price and asked him to come back at noon today. Then I went to the police and arranged for these two sheriffs to be waiting with me."

The young man held his head up, and his mouth formed a challenging sneer. "I didn't steal those pictures. They were given to me." Then he pointed his finger at Maria. "By her!"

Despite the confusion and the stares of everyone in the room, Maria found her voice. She faced Rembrandt with confidence. Many things began to make sense to her now.

"This is Freeda's cousin," she declared. "Or so she told me." Freeda hunched down in her seat, looking like a cornered rabbit. "I only saw him a couple of times, sneaking out of the yard or whispering with Freeda. I never spoke to him. Whenever I saw him, he pulled his cap down over his eyes and went off."

"He's not my cousin," Freeda protested. "Just a fellow I met at the market. We're friends, that's all."

"Don't say anything else!" the young man hissed.

Maria stepped closer to him and pointed to his jacket. "I see you're missing a button," she said. The apprentices strained forward and the sheriffs looked at their captive's coat. "They are odd ones," she added, "shaped more like wooden barrels than round buttons."

"What's that got to do with stolen prints?" van Dyke interrupted.

"Well, someone was in the shed the day Domingo died," Maria said. "I remember now that I noticed shoe prints in the dirt. It was a day when none of us were around. Hendrickje had to go out and she sent me to market because Titus was off with his friends. Rembrandt was busy finishing the etchings with the apprentices. Freeda was down here on her own."

"I'm confused," whined van Dyke.

"While everyone was away, someone went into the shed, poisoned Domingo, and buried him in the compost pile."

"Who's Domingo?" van Dyke asked in alarm.

"Be quiet!" Rembrandt yelled at the dealer.

"When I found Domingo, I also found something else on the ground near the compost pile." Maria reached into her pocket, relieved that the forgotten object was still there. She held it up. "A strange, barrel-shaped button!"

Titus turned from the button Maria held to the young man's jacket. "Why, even the threads match! But why would he poison Domingo?"

Maria didn't look at Freeda. The girl who had accused her only minutes ago would now be the one with no defense. "Perhaps he needed to get rid of Domingo so Freeda wouldn't be afraid to go into the shed and leave the items she stole for him." There was a gleam of understanding in Rembrandt's eyes. Freeda buried her head in her hands. "And with Domingo gone, there was less chance that I would go into the shed and accidentally find the things that Freeda hid there for this man to sell in town."

"It wasn't much," Freeda moaned. "Just a few things you'd never miss."

"Don't say anything!" the young man shouted. "You'll land us both in jail!"

"The master pays me so little," she complained. "It isn't fair. I do everything in this household. Everything!"

19

Taking a Chance

ry, yellow leaves rustled against the parlor window. Maria marveled at the change in the weather. The summer had been nearly as hot as Brazil, but by the time they had celebrated the Jewish New Year in September, there had already been a dramatic change.

"It seems your thoughts have flown out the window," Titus teased. Maria turned her attention back to the gathering in the room she had slept in just a few short weeks ago.

"I was thinking how much the weather has changed," she responded, "and how many other things in my life, as well." She looked across the room at her parents. "Every time I look up and see you, I have to blink to be sure I'm not dreaming."

Hendrickje sat close to the fire with a gray wool blanket over her lap. Her new baby daughter slept peacefully in a cradle next to her, and Hendrickje rocked it dreamily with her hand. "So many miracles in such a short time," she said.

Rabbi Menasseh looked content. "We have welcomed a new year, seen the reuniting of a family, and experienced the blessing of a new life. Truly, God smiles upon us."

"And don't forget the wonders of a new mother bursting with good health!" Rembrandt added. "Hendrickje has recovered so quickly. I'm convinced it's because she's been resting so well. Once we sent Freeda away, I was determined to replace her with someone dependable. The new housekeeper is a tireless worker."

"She is a wonder," Hendrickje agreed. "She helps with little Cornelia, cooks, keeps the house in perfect order, and yet always seems to be at my side whenever I need her."

Maria tensed at the mention of Freeda.

"You were quite forgiving of the last girl," Matilda Ben Israel remarked. "You could have sent her and her partner to jail."

Rembrandt shrugged. "What's the point? The things she took are gone and neither of them had a guilder to repay me. The young man went back to his family's farm and took Freeda with him. At least we've seen the last of them."

Rabbi Menasseh held his wineglass aloft. "Here's to forgiveness, in the spirit of the Lord."

Titus joined in the toast, raising his cup of tea. "Here's to Hendrickje and my beautiful sister, Cornelia."

Matilda added the Hebrew blessing, *"L'Chaim!"*

"To life!" Rembrandt echoed. "And I've determined it will be a debt-free one from now on. I won't have Cornelia growing up without some financial security. After all, there's a dowry to be thought of!"

Titus looked proudly at his father. "Did you know Father has just sold a painting to a collector in Italy?"

"At least in Italy they appreciate my work," Rembrandt grumbled. "I've been paid ten times what the miserly Amsterdamers would give me." He took a long drink of wine. "I'll give every guilder of it to Heer Thyss and hope he agrees to give me a few more months to pay off the rest of my debt. There are bound to be more commissions."

"And what are your plans, Abraham?" the rabbi asked. "Will you continue to make so many voyages now that you've found Maria?"

Her father shifted his long legs and settled back in the blue chair. "I began trading in tobacco so I could search for the children, although it was hard to leave Eva alone. Now it would be more difficult to leave her and Maria. And there are always risks in these long voyages." He stood and walked to the window. "I have given some thought to processing tobacco here in Amsterdam, but I've made no firm decisions."

Maria knew what her father left unsaid. "We still must find Isobel," she said softly. "There's more chance of getting news here."

The new housekeeper entered. She was a middle-aged woman in a neat brown dress and a spotless white apron. She passed around another tray of cakes, but everyone declined except Titus.

"You know," Abraham said, "I traveled to many colonies to purchase tobacco, and I always tried to find the girls. I was even in Recife once, but I never located any of the monasteries or heard a word about kidnapped children."

Rabbi Menasseh folded his hands in his lap. "Maria's escape is truly remarkable. It's frightening to realize there are so many others still held."

"Will they ever find their families again?" Hendrickje asked.

"We're trying to make contact with the Portuguese in Recife," the rabbi said. "We'll do everything we can to get those children back. Finding their families will be another matter."

Maria felt an overwhelming sadness. She often dreamed of her friends at the monastery and wondered how they were surviving. But, she had to admit, it wasn't nearly as often as she dreamed of her sister.

"Thank you for a lovely dinner," Eva said, "but we really must go. Hendrickje needs to rest, and we have a long walk home."

Titus helped Maria with her new cloak. Her parents had ordered a wardrobe of clothes, but Maria liked the long blue cloak the best. It was of thick wool lined with a soft red fabric. It kept her warm from head to foot and was so bright and cheerful. It was exactly the opposite of the drab frock she had worn at the monastery. She had allowed her mother to choose the cloth for her outfits but had made her promise not to pick anything brown.

Maria patted Cornelia's tiny back and kissed Hendrickje on the cheek before leaving. She couldn't come to visit as often now that the weather was so cold.

Maria and her parents crossed the canal, pushing against the stiff breeze. A flower vendor huddled at the foot of the bridge, warming his hands over a small stove.

"Let's bring home some flowers," Eva suggested. "These must be the last of the season." She looked through the array of flowers, trying to decide between a potted plant that might last the winter and the few cut flowers that were offered.

As her mother debated with herself, Maria observed a tired-looking young man approach the vendor. He wore a thin black cloak, heavy leather boots, and baggy breeches. He looked like many of the sailors and dockworkers who could be found at the fringes of the marketplace, unloading ships or scrubbing the decks and railings with fresh water.

"Pardon me," he said in strangely accented Dutch. "I am looking for the home of the Portuguese rabbi. Can you direct me?"

The vendor pointed across the canal and the young man moved off. As her mother paid for a thick bouquet of orange sunflowers, Maria watched his receding back. He walked with his toes pointed out, planting each foot heavily, as if he were expecting the street to move suddenly. He must be a sailor just off a boat, she guessed. He hasn't quite gotten his balance on land.

As she walked on with her parents, she couldn't help wondering what his mission was. He was definitely not Portuguese, as his accent proved. Nor was he Dutch. He didn't know Rabbi Menasseh, for he didn't ask for him by name. What would bring him straight from a tiring voyage in search of a rabbi? She felt he might have some new information, but she couldn't tell her parents of her feelings. Logically, it made no sense. Still, she couldn't let him go without questioning him.

"I've forgotten my gloves!" she exclaimed. She held her cloak closed, hoping her parents wouldn't notice the bulge of her pocket. "You go on ahead. I'll run back and meet you at home."

"We'll come with you," her father said.

"It's much too cold," she argued. "I'll be along shortly."

Her parents hesitated but finally gave in. "Don't stay long," her father cautioned. "It gets dark so early now." She watched them walk away before turning and hurrying down the street.

When she caught up to the sailor, he was standing on the street, looking in confusion at the narrow houses. She hesitated. *What am I thinking of? I don't know anything about this sailor or his mission.* But an inner feeling urged her to act. She pulled her hood up, partially concealing her face.

"Excuse me," she called out. "Did you say you were looking for the rabbi?"

The young man looked at her gratefully. "I seem to be hopelessly lost."

"Rabbi Ben Israel lives on this street," she assured him, "but he isn't at home right now. I could take you to him, if it's important."

He shook his head in exasperation. "I've barely got my balance on shore and I've done more walking than I thought to do in a month!" He gave a short bow as Maria took her gloves from her cloak pocket and pulled them on. "My name is Jean-Pierre Baptiste," he said. "I am a French sailor from the *Sainte Cathérine*. We've had a most unusual voyage, battling with a Spanish caravel and ending up rescuing a group of Jewish colonists from Recife, Brazil."

Maria nearly gasped, but tried to act calm. "Do you have news of the passengers from *The Valck*?"

The young man looked surprised. "How did you know? That's the first ship they traveled on. I've been

given a letter from one of the passengers and have
spent the day on a fruitless search for a man named
Abraham Ben Lazar. It seems no one has heard of such
a gentleman. I thought perhaps the rabbi might be able
to help me."

Maria could barely contain her excitement, but recognized the danger of betraying her father. The sailor
could be lying. He could be a spy sent from the emissary from Portugal. She had to be cautious and judge
carefully.

"Let's find a warm place where we can talk," she
offered. "Maybe I can help you."

The sailor accompanied her to a small pancake shop
not far from her parents' house. They sat at a round
wooden table close to the fire and ordered hot choco-
late. The young man draped his cloak over an empty
chair and helped Maria with hers. They faced each
other over two steaming mugs of frothy cocoa.

"You've told me who the letter is for but not who it's
from," she prodded.

"It all started when our ship prepared to take on
supplies in Cuba," he began. "When we approached
the cove we surprised a Spanish caravel. It bore no flag
and we were certain it was manned by privateers. The
captain ordered us to fire before it attacked us. There
was a brief battle, and they quickly set sail. We were
cautious when we sent men ashore, in case there were
Spaniards lying in wait for us, but that was not what
we found."

Maria tried to imagine the battle between the ships
and wondered where Isobel fit it. If the privateers had
sailed away, did that mean her sister was still captive?

He cupped his large, callused hands around the hot

mug and took a long swallow. "When we headed for the village we saw that a stockade just off the path was barred from the outside. We did not know what to expect, but we swung the gate open and came face to face with a small group of families who had been locked inside by the privateers."

She felt filled with hope. How had she guessed he would have word of Isobel? She sipped at her cocoa to calm herself. "Why were they made prisoners?"

The young man looked at her closely and seemed momentarily distracted from his story. "There were twenty-three Jews there," he continued. "Adults and children of all ages, even a baby. They had been kidnapped from *The Valck* while trying to travel to Amsterdam. The privateers planned to sell them to the Inquisition for a hefty payment." He smiled proudly. "But we changed their plans."

"If you've brought these people with you, I'm surprised the city isn't filled with the news," she said.

"We haven't brought them here," Baptiste said, emphasizing the last word. Maria's heart sank. "Which is why I carry this letter." He pulled a folded paper from his vest pocket. "Our merchant ship carried passengers and cargo bound for New Amsterdam in the Americas. Captain de la Motthe was willing to take these families on the voyage there, but not without guarantees of payment."

The sailor's pride of a moment before gave way to embarrassment. "You cannot blame the captain," he protested, although Maria hadn't made any accusation. "The ship was full, and there was a shortage of supplies. After we discovered the families in the stockade, the captain was afraid the caravel would return for them. We couldn't stay to stock up on fresh food or water."

Baptiste seemed uncomfortable under Maria's steady gaze. "I know it was wrong, but it was the captain's business. He negotiated a very steep fare with the spokesman of the group."

"But they couldn't have had a guilder among them," Maria guessed. "If they already paid for their passage on *The Valck* and then were captured by the privateers, how could they have had anything of value?"

"Of course you're right," he agreed. "That is why we only took them as far as New Amsterdam, our first stop. There was an auction of the few belongings they still possessed, but it wasn't enough to meet their debt. Finally, an agreement was worked out. A portion of the fare was raised and given to the captain. The rest of us in the crew agreed to wait until next year for our share of the payment. Still, there was no possibility that the captain would carry these people on a second journey here."

"But what of the letter?" Maria interrupted. "How did you come to be entrusted with it?"

"The day after we sailed out of Cuba," Baptiste recalled, "I met a young girl who was traveling with the Jewish families we rescued. She told me she was searching for her family and I made the foolish mistake of teasing her." He shook his head. "I couldn't have known how serious her situation was, but the joke was not taken well. In fact, she refused to speak to me for several days." His face brightened. "But time helps all fools. Soon, we became better friends than we might have otherwise. I got to know all the new passengers,

but especially this one. Her name was Isobel Ben Lazar."

Maria felt her hair tingle on her head. If the sailor's
story was true, her sister was safe in New Amsterdam,
living with a group of Jewish families. She determined
to test Baptiste with the two things Cado had told her.

"What did the girl look like?" she asked.

"She was a thin, dark-haired girl," the sailor said,
"with large brown eyes that always looked a bit sad."
He paused and then added one last detail. It was just
what Maria had been waiting to hear. "There was just
one odd thing about her." He smiled. "Her hair was
cut short as a boy's. Just chopped off clean. She said
the cook on *The Valck* had done it to try to disguise her
as a cabin boy so the privateers wouldn't find her." He
looked more intently at Maria. "If her hair had been
longer, I would say she was the image of you."

She nearly shouted that Isobel was her sister. She
twisted a fold of her dress in her hands, trying to steady
herself to ask one last important question.

"I suppose her hair was too short for ornaments,"
she commented, trying to sound uninterested.

"I had almost forgotten!" Baptiste said excitedly.
"She had these two silver hair combs, very intricate in
their design. She told me her sister had given them to
her when they parted ways in Recife. She kept them
hidden from everyone—the privateers, the cook, and
even the family that took her in. But when the court
in New Amsterdam ordered the auction to pay the captain for the Jews' passage, she offered them for sale. No
one knew she had them, so she didn't have to give
them up. But I guess she felt she owed these families
something. They had taken her in as if she were their

own. She simply walked up to the auctioneer and handed him those combs."

I told Isobel the combs could be sold if that was the only way to get home, Maria thought. Did she think there was no hope of ever getting to Amsterdam? Or had she found a new home?

"There was quite a scene when she gave them away," the sailor continued. "But she didn't lose them in the end."

"But you said they were sold," Maria reminded him.

"That's true. A colonist bought them and paid a good price, too. But she didn't keep them. She offered them back to Isobel as a gift. The other colonists followed the woman's example and returned all the belongings to the Jewish families. It was a generous act on their part and showed the new arrivals they were welcome in the colony." He chuckled. "As short as her hair was, I never saw Isobel without those combs after that day. I'd bet she sleeps with them!" He looked at Maria questioningly. "Can you help me deliver the letter?"

Maria leaned across the table and held out her hand. "Thank you for what you've done. I'll take my sister's letter."

Baptiste was startled. A slow grin spread across his face. "Of course! Of course! You have to be Maria!"

She took the letter and excitedly reached for her cloak. She tossed a coin on the table and pulled the sailor out the door. "You've got to meet my parents," she told him. "Come on!"

They rushed through the streets, laughing at their breathlessness. Maria laughed with pure joy. Isobel was

not in Amsterdam, but she was safe. She was found.
She knew her parents would find a way to bring them
all together. She burst into the house, leading Baptiste
by the hand.

"Mama! Papa! I have news!"

20

Setting Sail

eel the wind," Abraham said. "It's a fair westerly breeze that will fill the sails and get our journey off to a smooth start. We're lucky in that."

Maria tried to keep pace with her father's hurried steps. It had been only ten days since Jean-Pierre Baptiste had brought Isobel's letter, but from the moment they learned she was in New Amsterdam, they began preparing to join her.

"I pray we'll have fair winds throughout the journey," Eva worried aloud. "It's a cold and stormy time to be voyaging so far."

It was hard to believe that her father had made arrangements so quickly, but there would be few ships sailing to the Americas later than this. They had all agreed they didn't want to wait until spring. Rugs, furniture, and dishes were sold to nearby dealers. Clothes, linens, and bedding were packed.

Abraham purchased many bolts of cloth to be sold to the colonists once they landed. "Cloth is a precious necessity in New Amsterdam," he said, feeling certain he could establish a good living selling fabric, buttons, and thread.

Maria watched a brilliant scarlet sun float up over the horizon. The last few days had been mild, almost making her forget there would be a cold winter ahead. She watched the marketplace stir to life. Farmers set up their stalls, and bakers and pancake sellers already called out their wares. Now, instead of peas, peppers, and other summer vegetables, the stalls were piled with turnips, squash, beets, and late-season crops.

"Should I purchase a few more loaves of bread before we go?" Eva asked.

Abraham laughed. "You've enough provisions for a journey twice as long as ours. Let's leave some food for those who stay behind!"

In the few months Maria had lived in Amsterdam, she never thought of it as her home. There was always something missing. But when she tried to make her goodbyes, she realized the feelings she had developed for her new friends. They had given her hope, and they had offered her love.

A familiar sound intruded on her thoughts. Tap, click, click. Tap, click, click.

"Rembrandt! Hendrickje!" she cried, embracing them. "And look, Mama, they've brought Cornelia." She looked quickly from the tiny infant swaddled in thick blankets to the others, but she hoped her eyes did not betray her disappointment. Titus had not come.

"We've come to see you off," Rembrandt said, "and wish you a safe voyage."

They moved closer to the docks, and Maria saw the swaying planks that led aboard the three ships that would depart together. Her stomach fluttered at the prospect of once again riding on a vessel that lurched with every swell of the sea. She tried to console herself with the thought that at the end of this journey she would find her sister.

Two more faces materialized out of the dim light. "It's the Ben Israels," Hendrickje said, smiling. "We'll give you a proper send-off yet."

"We were afraid we'd be too late," the rabbi puffed. "We nearly ran all the way. I'm too old for such exertion!"

The rabbi handed Abraham a heavy package. "Prayer books," he declared. "There are at least twenty-three Jews in New Amsterdam already. So, you'll need prayer books."

Abraham embraced Rabbi Menasseh warmly. "They'll be put to good use. I've brought as many of my books as I could. It will be a new beginning for us. Once we set foot in the colony, I shall become Abraham Ben Lazar once again."

Hendrickje gave Eva the basket she had been carrying. She pushed back some of the straw to reveal several sealed jars. "These are some of the vegetables from Maria's garden. She barely got to taste the results of all her work."

Maria thought of the hours she had spent tending the garden and playing with Domingo. He was another friend she was leaving behind. She looked across the brightening marketplace, remembering her wild chase when the rat had escaped. She could picture his tiny legs racing around baskets and stalls, hopping across the cobblestones. But today there was someone else she had hoped to see in the marketplace.

Rembrandt cleared his throat. "I've brought something, too. Not nearly as tasty as Hendrickje's vegetables." Cornelia started to fuss, and Hendrickje put her finger against the baby's mouth. Strong sucking sounds made everyone smile.

"Don't talk of eating," she joked. "She's always hungry!"

Rembrandt handed Maria a small packet wrapped in brown paper and tied with string. She set her bundles down and untied it. Other passengers walked by to board the ship, and Abraham looked back anxiously. "Better hurry," he cautioned. "Everyone's boarding."

Maria pulled an etching from the wrapping. It was her own likeness, from the series she and Titus had taken to van Dyke. The print was signed and numbered 150. "But I thought this was sold."

"I saved it for you," the painter said. "After all, you deserve some reward for all that sitting."

"Perr-fectly still!" chimed a voice.

"Titus!" she cried. "I thought you weren't coming."

He wrapped his arms around Maria and gave her a long hug. When he released her, she saw he held something in each hand. "I had to stop and get something first," he explained. He handed her a lumpy paper packet. "These are tulip bulbs. Plant them as soon as you arrive in New Amsterdam, and when the snow melts you'll have Amsterdam blossoms. They'll bloom every year."

She reached into her cloak and placed her polished conch shell in Titus's hand. "When you hold it up to your ear, you can hear the sound of the ocean. Remember that it's only an ocean in a seashell that's between us."

"No more goodbyes," Abraham declared, "or our ship will be saying goodbye to us!"

Maria picked up her things. "When I first arrived

here I hadn't achieved my dream, for Isobel was lost and I didn't know how I would find her or my parents. I felt as if I had put only one foot ashore." Everyone looked solemn as she spoke, but then she laughed aloud. "Now I wish I didn't have to put either foot on one of these ships. One foot ashore may be better than two feet on deck! And what about my stomach? Where shall I put that?"

"Speaking of your stomach, there's one last thing," Titus said, and he handed her a warm, sweet-smelling roll of paper. "It's a pancake! You can't leave Amsterdam without eating at least one hot pancake!"

Maria hugged Titus, her bundles squashed between them. She took one last, long look at each of the faces before her. Then she turned toward the ship, toward Isobel, and toward the certainty of planting two feet on a distant shore.

Temple Israel
Minneapolis, Minnesota

IN MEMORY OF
ROSE SCHLEIFF
FROM
CARYL & LARRY ABDO